WHAT SHE DIDN'T KNOW

Patricia E. Gitt

Print edition ISBN 978-1-7341584-9-6

Ebook edition ISBN 978-1-7345478-0-1

This book was printed in the United States of America

Also by Patricia E. Gitt:

New York City Mysteries:

CEO

ASAP – as soon as possible - A settling of scores

TBD – to be determined - A game changer

FYI – An unintended consequence

Published by:

Athena Book Publishing
New York, New York
Athenabookpublishing.com

Dedication

"To Wendy H. Jones, crime writer extraordinaire, for her inspiration, guidance and friendship."

Acknowledgements

I am very lucky to count celebrated authors among my friends. The following have kept me from permanent writer's block: Jane Thornley, Catherine Kullmann, Bonnie Milani, Valerie Keogh, MG Crisci and AB Gibson.

Other friends have kindly acted as beta readers and were ready to put me back on track with their helpful thoughts on aspects of this tale: Mary Karpin, Elinor Ruskin and Angela Knauss.

Special thanks to Sharon Johnson who kept me digging into these characters and moving forward, even when I didn't know where the next chapter would go.

In addition I would like to thank Lawrence W. Kreutzberg for his introduction to a Life Insurance Agent's responsibilities. The embellishments are all mine.

Contents

"It is easier to live through someone else than to become complete yourself."

Betty Friedan

Prologue

2018

The morning sun sat low in the sky with enough strength to add sparkle to the dense, snow covered landscape. As the guide held out his hand and assisted Sally to step from the zodiac to the shore, he reminded her to keep to the path marked by little flags.

"It's still early so the snow on the path is packed, unlike a bit later where your boots will sink, making your walk more difficult," he cautioned.

The lecture aboard the excursion ship the evening before reminded passengers to let the penguins continue on their way, and if one crossed their path they were to wait until they had passed. "Oh my," Sally said as she watched the little oval body with very short legs waddle from side to side as it moved from the right of her path across to the other side. "How sweet," she said to herself as she continued to watch the little fellow move on his way. No travelogue on this journey to Antarctica prepared her for the personality of the penguins.

The path she was on led up to a rise and on arrival she heard a guide addressing the small group of fellow travelers from the previous zodiac landing. "If you look

Patricia E. Gitt

closely, that jumble of rocks are independent nesting sites built of pebbles. Watch as the female sits on her eggs, while her mate moves from this colony, across our path to the colony on the lower part of this slope."

"The little fellow is stealing a pebble from that nest," remarked one of the travelers.

"Notice that he climbed up an unoccupied side of that nest so as not to anger one of the other birds," answered the guide.

Sally watched as the penguin, the pebble held tightly in his small beak, hobbled down the pile, back across her path and worked his way up to his mate. She couldn't get enough of the sight. This was a trip she had dreamed of since the fourth grade.

Looking below the path she gazed out to the inlet surrounded by glaciers and watched another zodiac arriving with a few more passengers from the ship. A short distance away sat the cruise ship waiting for their return. As she looked beyond the inlet to the channel she saw aqua tinted ice floating on the current, moving past other outcrops of snow covered land in the distance. Then she turned her gaze back to the upper penguin colony, looking for Tyler. "Now where did he go off to," she said quietly. Sally smiled as she spotted her husband behind the larger bird colony, taking one photo after another. While he paid attention to cautions to stay within the marked areas, he often wandered away to get that special shot.

Sally's smile caught short when she saw her husband stumble, quickly recover his balance and move away for

2

another scenic shot. *Oh shit, did I pour too much of the potion into this morning's coffee? I didn't want his nicotine withdrawal to interfere with this fabulous first day ashore.*

Tyler was a wonderful husband who, wanting to give her the honeymoon they never had, made this lifelong dream come true. Sally realized she was one very lucky gal.

Chapter 1

2017

"They're dressed like dolls," murmured Sally as she watched her husband's eight-year-old young son and ten-year-old daughter approach the car.

"What did you say, sweetheart?" Tyler asked, not turning to hear his wife's reply, as he stepped out and greeted two very clean, well-dressed kids.

She watched as Judy and Billy rushed into her husband's open arms with words tumbling over one another, looking like any kids happy to see their father.

"Hi Sally," a smiling Judith Grace sang out as she stepped into the back seat with her younger brother, William John, jumping in behind her.

"Judy and Billy, I have surprises," Sally said and turning around handed each child a small shopping bag.

Screams of delight echoed in the family car as Judy opened hers first, withdrawing a colorful cotton skirt and matching pink t-shirt. "How did you know I needed something to wear at the club," she all but cried.

"Me too," Billy jumped in as he saw a new pair of chinos and white t-shirt with the country club logo on it. Sally knew it probably wasn't the normal reaction of an eight-year-old, but she also knew the home they lived in.

"I was washing your other clothes, you know, the ones your dad bought last summer, and knew you wanted to look your best for your friends."

"Kids, Sally made Judy's skirt and your pants, Billy. You should thank her." Tyler loved his wife more and more each day. And when she bonded with his children, there was nothing he wouldn't do for her.

"Oh, Sally, long pants, how did you know I don't want to wear kids' clothes anymore?" Billy cried.

Sally settled back for the drive to the country club, pleased that by now, four years later, she understood Judy and Billy. If she could mother these two who were starving for affection, she knew that the child she and Tyler were hoping for would be safe.

* * *

The noisy group tumbled out of the car with Tyler trailing behind, carefully folding the clothes Judy and Billy wore earlier that day over his arm.

"Why don't you go upstairs and clean up. I'll bring these up and you can look as crisp and clean as you did when we picked you up this morning," Sally called after the two children racing up the stairs. It had been a good day, with Judy taking a tennis lesson and Billy learning to dive at the pool.

"Sweetheart, they sound like kids around you. I remember the two solemn faces we met today. In fact, every time we pick them up." With that, Tyler drew his wife into his arms for a warm hug. "I wish they could stay with us. You'd make us one happy family."

"Was life with Victoria always without humor? You never mentioned what it was like to be married to her."

"Truthfully, I worked not only to pay the bills, but to stay away. The only pleasure after Judy was born, then Billy, was my weekends with them."

"Didn't your wife join you?"

"No. Thank God."

The sounds of footsteps rushing down the stairs stopped Sally from continuing the conversation. She was the reason Tyler divorced Victoria. Even after four years of marriage, he never shared all he endured. She, however, saw the cruelty of Victoria during and after the divorce. It still gave her chills.

With the kids in the backyard, Sally picked up the towels and clothes left in the upstairs guest room and gathered them for washing. As she reached the bottom of the staircase, the sight of a black aberration, the thorn in her side, about to open one of her kitchen cabinets, stopped her cold.

"Victoria, can I get something for you?" Sally said in a calm controlled voice. The only tone she would let herself use in this woman's presence.

A thin hand capped in crimson nail polish fell to her side. "I was looking for a glass. The drive over made me thirsty."

Sally quickly moved the anorexic woman away from the cabinet in which she stored her homemade tonics and creams. "I keep the glasses here, near the sink." Reaching for a glass, she filled it from the tap. "I didn't hear you ring."

"I didn't want to disturb you. Anyway, the door was open."

Right, you snoop. Trying to find something else to hold against me. Won't you ever stop? "We're lucky. The water here is pure and tastes as clear as that you find in commercially bottled brands."

Sally watched the woman take the glass, barely sip and hand it back with a crimson imprint on its rim. Sally placed the glass in the sink and seeing Victoria turn as if to head for the back door, said, "Your shirt is really lovely. It's silk, isn't it?" stopping the woman in her tracks. "Since I just painted the back hall, I am sure you wouldn't want to get it stained. Let's go out the way you came in. The children are around back."

"You aren't giving your gardener direction. These bushes need trimming," was the flatly stated comment as Victoria led the way around the side of the house. She knew the way. It wasn't her first visit. Tyler had the kids every other Sunday, and Victoria made sure she picked them up after a day with her ex.

"Tyler does the lawn and trims the bordering bushes. I am sure he will get around to it in time."

The sounds of cheerful children could be heard from the back yard, as Tyler asked one question after another and

Patricia E. Gitt

the kids rushed to see who could give a funnier answer, with the smell of hamburgers cooking on the grill adding to the family scene.

To her continual dismay, Sally watched the children's automatic reaction to their mother's appearance. The laughing stopped, they sat up straight, and with ingrained training, Judy picked up a napkin and tucked it into the collar of her dress, while Billy quickly tucked a napkin into his shirt.

"Victoria, you are a half hour early. Judy and Billy haven't finished eating," said Tyler, focused on his grill and not the object of his comment. "Why not sit over there out of the sun. I can grill something for you if you wish."

"No. I'll wait." And a day of family fun ended.

Chapter 2

Screams of challenges were thrown around by four excited kids as the game of badminton progressed. The men coaching watched as they swatted, ducked and dove to capture the elusive feathered shuttlecock.

"Ryan, I am so glad you decided to bring Jane and Mark over. Judy and Billy needed some normal family time," Tyler said to his brother.

"A really great idea. I forget to invite us over, and this weather makes for a perfect day out of the City. I for one am glad you decided to commute from Great Neck to New York. When you and Sally finally finish this house and start raising kids, we can have our own family day camp."

Sally didn't notice her husband's frown. She was too busy imagining the scene Ryan was suggesting. Family. Everything she ever wanted.

A crunching sound brought her back to earth with a jolt. A car was pulling up in the driveway. The quick glance at her watch told her that Victoria was almost an hour early. Lately she managed to be inconveniently early, but never by the same amount of time.

Quick steps brought Sally to the corner of the house before the woman could sneak in the front door. "Victoria, I was just going to make some coffee, would you like some?"

Victoria tried to hide her displeasure at being met by the woman who stole her husband and ruined her life. "Tea."

"I have green tea. Would that be all right?"

"No. Coffee, black will be fine."

"Well don't let me keep you. Everyone is around back."

"What on earth are the children wearing," Victoria snapped as she rounded the corner of the house.

Ryan, never understanding how his brother could have dated, let alone married this woman, stood up as she walked into the yard. "Hello, Victoria. It's a weekend and everyone is dressed for fun."

"You're early, Victoria," Tyler said, trying to keep Ryan from more of his ex's sharp tongue. "We saved you a seat. It will be a while before the kids will be ready to leave. Dinner isn't quite ready."

Sally wasn't in a hurry to return to the group but felt guilty leaving Tyler and Ryan to deal with their visitor. By now she had learned how to deflect and change the contentious mood sparked by the woman's presence.

Straightening up, she picked up the tray with coffee pot, cups, cream and sugar, and walked out the back door. "Victoria, may I pour you a cup? You drink it black, if I remember," Sally said as she set the tray near a stack of paper plates, napkins and plastic forks.

The dark shoulder length hair barely moved as the woman gave a brief nod.

"Ryan?"

"Sally, sit, you've done enough today, what with lunch and snacks for the kids. I'll pour," he said, taking the coffee pot from her hand.

"Okay, dinner coming up," Tyler announced and began to place hamburgers on the grill, and the buns to warm on the shelf. "Kids, dinner in a few minutes, you'd better wash up."

Jane and Mark walked up to their father, and looking at Victoria, politely said their hellos. Judy and Billy rushed into the house without pausing to greet their mother.

"Victoria, I understand you may be taking up bridge," Ryan said, turning the woman's attention away from the departing children. "If you like, I can recommend a book I used when I thought I might like to join a bridge club."

"No, I am taking a course at the local high school. It doesn't begin until September."

"Do you play any games with Judy and Billy? We play monopoly and banana grams," Ryan continued.

Sally listened as her brother-in-law tried to distract the woman from her usual caustic comments. He was a wonderful father and she knew how much he missed his wife, who died over a year ago. Sally was forever grateful to Gloria for making her feel part of the Scott family, and how she had tried to prepare her for the difficult road

Patricia E. Gitt

ahead. At first she hadn't believed that anyone Tyler married could be all that bad. But then Gloria had said, "If looks or acid tongue could kill, Victoria would be serving a life sentence in prison." Now, Ryan focused solely on work and his kids. They were his life. She was glad he was reconnecting with Tyler. Both men needed one another, as much as they needed their children.

"No. I let William play his video game, and Judith prefers to read," Victoria said, her statement without a hint of personal interest in her children's activities. *I'll bet she doesn't even know what books or games her kids liked in their solitary lives*, Sally thought.

Once the kids settled around the table Victoria was ignored. A new game was started, the old standby, geography... It was one way Tyler tried to open up the world for his highly restricted kids. Court ruling in the divorce prevented him from taking the kids out of the area. So he was limited to one day every other weekend, and the occasional weekday dinner.

Someday, Sally prayed, let Vicious Victoria find someone else to harass.

12

Chapter 3

"Something smells delicious," a tired but happy Tyler said while snuggling Sally in a hug.

"When you told me you were going to be leaving work early, I made your favorite veal scallopini and apple pie for dessert." She loved cooking for her husband, he always let her know her efforts were appreciated, not only in commenting on ingredients or texture of a dish, but by savoring every bite.

"Let's have a drink first. I want to forget the day and enjoy my wife," Tyler said and gave Sally a deep passionate kiss.

As she looked up into her husband's eyes Sally thought how lucky she was to be loved by this man. "You pour," she replied.

Tyler made them both martinis, he needed something stronger than a glass of wine. Sally walked over to him, reached for a glass, and nestled close on the sofa in front of the living room fireplace.

"Sigh," was the satisfied sound Tyler made and placed his arm around Sally's shoulders.

"Was it a particularly difficult day, darling?"

"No, but tense. I've told you that I just signed a major account for the firm. Mr. Delroy, he's the partner in charge of new business, praised me at a meeting."

"But that's wonderful," Sally exclaimed.

"Yes, but every time he singles me out for praise, that Warren Lazar drills me with those cold hard eyes."

"He's just jealous. Can't you ignore him? It isn't like he can hurt you."

"It's just that he's sneaky enough to sabotage me if he gets the chance. So I am always on alert."

"Well then, I have some news. Your proposals for those two prospective clients are done, and so are the Club's minutes. I seemed to be on a roll today."

"You know I hired you as my executive assistant at the agency because your portfolio contained copies of the most professionally written company reports. It took me a week more to fall madly in love with you," Tyler said hugging his wife even closer. "A refill, Honeybunch?"

"Mm. Only if you don't mind waiting for dinner."

"One more drink and I'll follow you into the kitchen. You are the best remedy for unwinding this hard-working man."

After the dishes were done, Sally led Tyler back to the living room with two cups of tea. It was a special blend that would further soothe her overworked husband. "Tyler, would you tell me what made you marry Victoria? There must have been some feelings, even love for you to take such a leap."

14

"Ah, after all these years, you still want to know?" Tyler moved over to the window, tea forgotten, and stared out at the side yard. Pulling an almost empty pack of cigarettes out of his shirt pocket, he turned back to face Sally. "I know you don't like me to smoke in the house."

Sally just gave him a tight-lipped smile that clearly showed her disapproval.

Turning back to the window, he muttered, "Right. Victoria. Marriage," he said, taking a deep drag on his cigarette.

"As you know, she worked in an expensive dress shop near my office. After work, I would sometimes meet Ryan for a drink. You know, to catch up on his growing family. Victoria came in one evening and seemed to be drawn to me. After I bought her a drink, she seemed to reappear frequently, and one day I asked her to dinner. A charming, sexy brunette, who paid attention to my every word. You can't imagine how attractive that was for someone focused only on his career."

"And you began a relationship!" Sally hoped he would continue. The picture he painted of his first wife was diametrically opposite the Victoria she knew.

"Well, sex. And it became a habit for me, until..."

"Until?"

"One evening she told me she was pregnant. And I proposed."

"Were you ever happy?"

15

Patricia E. Gitt

"Sort of, until we moved to the suburbs and she started spending more money than I earned. That need for money, along with her lack of physical interest in me, kept me working longer hours."

Sally rushed to wrap her arms around her husband. Leaning her head against his back, she wondered how one woman could destroy someone so sensitive and loving. Tyler, feeling her closeness, turned and pulled Sally into his arms. One thing that never changed in a year of dating and the four years of marriage was their instant chemistry. Words weren't needed. Just the closeness of their bodies that soon had them burning with sexual hunger.

"Mm, lack of interest doesn't seem to be your problem. Let's do something to satisfy your curiosity," Tyler murmured and ground out his cigarette in the nearby ashtray.

"You know what they say about that cat? Curiosity brought him back," Sally said, giggling as they headed for the bedroom.

Chapter 4

"Sally, this is terrific. I want to see the whole house. I can't imagine taking an entire year out of my life to tackle a job this size."

Laughing felt good. Jeanne could always make her feel special. "Actually, I enjoyed it. It was good exercise. I had Billie Holiday and Nat King Cole for company and could sing out loud without disturbing Tyler. Wear old, now paint covered jeans and t-shirts large enough for King Kong. Not only did Tyler always say my singing sounded like a screeching cat, he hated me in anything loose fitting or messy.

"Let's start upstairs. I want to show you the hint of color I used in each room. It's subtle, but when you stand in the hall with the doors open and the sun shining through the windows, it looks like I planted a garden of flowers."

The tour didn't take long as only a small bedroom, the master bedroom and bath, and a sparsely furnished guest room were painted. "Sally, I hesitate to ask, but why is the smaller bedroom white? Is it going to be a home gym? I see Tyler's weights over in the corner."

Sally's eyes misted, and reaching for a hankie turned away, hoping Jeanne didn't notice. As quickly as they started, they ceased. "That's the nursery. I didn't want to pick a color until I knew whether I was expecting a boy or girl."

"Okay, a drink. The sun must be over the yardarm somewhere in the world," Jeanne said as she led Sally back downstairs and into the kitchen.

With the mood changed by thoughts of a drink, Sally brightened. "I have a new delicious cocktail…it's a favorite of my mom's and right out of the 60s."

"Let me guess, a Sidecar?"

"Yes. How about it? Vodka, Cointreau and lemon juice."

Settled into the dining nook, Sally saw Jeanne's wrinkled brow and knew she was about to be put under the third degree. They had been roommates when Sally first came to work in the city. At times Jeanne could read her like a book. "Out with it. What did I do now?" Sally asked.

After a sip of her drink, Jeanne gave Sally a puzzled look and paused to gather her thoughts. "Well, how much longer will it take to paint that white room, the upstairs hallway and extra bathroom?"

"I also have to finish the downstairs hallway, and laundry room," Sally added.

"What is your end date? I know you from before this marriage and you have the mind of an accountant, plotting and planning everything. You do have an end date?"

"Yes, I guess. Let's see, it's July now, I should be finished by September. Why?"

"How about you? Have you even thought of what you are going to do? You can't stay buried out here in suburbia where husbands park their families while they play around in the city?"

"Don't be cruel. Tyler isn't like that. He's devoted to me."

"Then why aren't you pregnant? Is he infertile? After you began painting this house did you stop having sex?"

"Stop it. Damn you, Jeanne. I went to the doctor and I'm fine. We screw like bunny rabbits. But I'm staying on the pill until I finish painting the house. I'm afraid of breathing in all those fumes while I'm pregnant." It still hurt to remember those missed opportunities when she was ready, but Tyler was off on another business trip. Sally couldn't hide her disappointment. "I guess it hasn't been our time to have children."

"Have you taken a good look in the mirror lately? I look at you and see a mere shadow of the strong-minded young woman I love like a sister. Please don't shut me out. In fact, maybe talking about you for a change will help clear your mind."

With a sigh, Sally held up her glass ready for a toast. "To the new Sally Compton Scott. Getting her back on track. Family and maybe job? Is that what you are driving at?"

"To Sally Compton Scott, liberated woman," Jeanne responded with a broad smile.

"Okay, now what, Ms. fixer of paint-smeared damsels?" Sally joked.

Patricia E. Gitt

"Let me take you out for lunch. I feel I've won a major argument and it doesn't matter to me what you decide to do. I've missed you. Let's not let so much time separate us again," Jeanne said.

Chapter 5

"I feel like a woman again," said Sally as she gazed into the bedroom mirror at the reflection of a blonde, with short curly hair, dressed in a pink chiffon dress, pivoting in heels she hadn't worn in years.

Feeling Tyler's arms around her reminded her of the days before they were married and just being in one another's presence had bonded them in love.

"Okay, Honeybunch, more of this later. We have reservations at the Club for eight. And dancing after."

"What's the occasion? Not that I'm complaining," Sally quipped.

"I have a surprise for you and want to make sure you are your most delightful self."

The restaurant was almost filled when they arrived, and Tyler spotted the table he reserved off to the side of the room. It overlooked the golf course and was as romantic as a country club restaurant could offer.

"You order for me," Sally said. "I'll be right back."

Rising as his wife left the table, Tyler began humming a tuneless sound. Everything would be perfect. He was sure Sally would love his surprise.

"Dinner was delicious. I will have to learn the chef's secret for making his swordfish so tender. I tend to dry it out."

"Honeybunch, I live with an exceptional cook. You could give lessons." With his glass of red wine in hand, Tyler smiled. "To my lovely wife. Best friend. And the most remarkable bundle of talents ever."

"Wow." Sally could barely stop blushing as she sipped her wine.

"My surprise," Tyler began. "Christmas will be our fifth wedding anniversary, and we have never had a honeymoon. So where do you want to go? Anywhere is fine with me if it makes you happy."

Stunned, Sally just sat and stared at her husband's smiling face.

"Honeybunch?" Tyler said breaking the silence. "Don't you want to travel? Celebrate our happiness?"

"It's just that I'm overwhelmed. I have been pinching pennies all this time knowing that we are living almost beyond your earnings. I don't know what to say."

"That is another reason I want us to go away. You deserve it."

"Can I think a bit? Maybe research some places I've always wanted to visit?"

Watching his wife's shock and hearing her truthful concerns for their finances made Tyler squirm. He was planning to find any amount needed to fulfill his promise.

"I think that is a wonderful idea. You do the research and this weekend we can go over your wish list."

* * *

"Jeanne, I called for some advice," Sally said at eight the following morning.

"Let me get my coffee. Okay, shoot."

"Tyler wants to take me on a honeymoon trip to any place I want. You know I've dreamed of going to Antarctica, visiting the White Continent. But, Jeanne, the trip I want to take is so very expensive."

"And good housewife that you are, you can't justify suggesting it," Jeanne said thoughtfully. "You do have a dilemma. Why not gather colorful brochures of several places, cook one of your delicious meals, and spread them out for discussion. Maybe he will lean toward a less expensive option, then your problems are solved."

"Perfect!" Hanging up, Sally thought of all those travelogues she had seen on the computer. *Yes, I will gather three for discussion and print out local histories. I won't worry about expenses until Tyler tells me his choice.*

* * *

Their coffee cups off to one side of the breakfast nook, and colorful printouts spread out on the table, Sally saw surprise on Tyler's face. "Honeybunch, you really did your research. But I want this to be a trip you want. So give me your reasons behind each of these choices."

With another sip of coffee for courage, Sally put down her mug and started with Malta, the island with a history of having been the crossroads of the southern European peninsula. "Remember the Crusaders?"

"Sure. Christians fighting the infidels who were invading England and France."

"Well, in 1565 when the Maltese people needed help to keep the Turks from invading their island, the Knights of Saint John, who owned the island, pleaded to the Pope for help. And the Pope sent the Crusaders. Not only were they successful in keeping Malta safe, the Crusaders stayed on, dropping their swords and shields, and helped fortify the island against further invasions. Eventually, they were absorbed into the order of the Knights of Saint John. But there is also the story my grandfather told me when I was a kid. He had been stationed in Malta to fight the Germans in WWII. And he said the lovely island had been practically destroyed. According to this brochure, there is a Museum commemorating the brave who fought during WWII, and I thought it would be nice to see it. You know, for my granddad."

"That's quite a story," Tyler said surprised by the amount of history that was behind Sally's choice. "Okay. And Bermuda?"

"Well, you love golf. And one of the hotels is known for its challenging golf course. I could even join you for a round. But only if you want. I can always sit on the beach." She was beginning to enjoy the experience of planning for fun, not another household project.

"If I remember, when you returned the golf cart at the club last year, you told me the man you handed the keys to asked how your game was. And you told him proudly that you had shot a 178. And he said…"

"Yea, yea, 'Those are bowling scores,' Sally said laughing at this often told tale whenever she said she might take up golf.

"And your third choice?"

Sally sat up a little straighter, and after caressing the computer printout, slid the papers across the table.

Tyler reached for the pages and seeing Antarctica, looked up. "This is a dream? One of long standing?" he asked, his eyes wide in surprise.

Sally nodded. "This is a dream of a lifetime."

"Sally? It's at the bottom of the world. Is this the one you really want?"

Nodding yes. *Don't plead, just explain.* "When I was in fourth grade I had an assignment to write a composition on Ernest Shackleton. After reading about his four expeditions and all he had to do to prepare for living in subzero weather, I imagined I had gone along with him."

"But that couldn't be why you'd travel all that way. Come on, Sally, what else?" This was beyond what he had expected. Experienced traveler that he was, he knew it would be prohibitively expensive.

"When I was researching something in high school, I came across a video of Antarctica. It was surreal.

Glaciers like white mountains. Ice flows with penguins jumping in and out of the water to feed. Whales and seals. But no people. It was as if a painter had drawn a landscape all in shades of white."

Sally watched as Tyler sat quietly. She knew him well enough to see his brain figuring the costs. It certainly wasn't something he'd expected. "Tyler? It can wait. You know, when our children are grown. After we've saved for it."

"No. Let me think a minute."

Sally began biting her bottom lip, a sure sign of nerves. It was too much. She should have picked Florence, Italy, or Paris.

"All my trips are arranged by the travel agency my firm uses. I'll call one of the agents I've worked with and see what he can come up with. Okay?" Tyler asked, hoping that there was some way he could give his wife her dream.

Breathing a sigh of relief, her humor restored, Sally knew it was the right thing to do. She shared most everything with this wonderful man, but not her dreams about becoming a CPA, traveling to the White Continent, or her wishes he would stop smoking. He had cut down to less than one pack a day to please her. But now she was beginning to suspect he had returned to his former three packs-a-day habit.

Chapter 6

He hadn't slept a wink and left earlier than usual, telling Sally he had an unexpected appointment to prepare for. Not to worry, it was a breakfast meeting. As he took his seat on the train he dialed his brother. "Ryan, I know I didn't wake you at six am, but I do hope I'm not interrupting something."

"No Tyler, the kids won't be up for half an hour. What can I do for you?"

"Could we meet for drinks after work. That little bar near your office would be fine," Tyler said.

"Sure. Six?"

After he hung up, Tyler hoped his older brother, with a keener mind for figuring out personal problems, would help him figure out how he was going to find a way to take Sally to Antarctica.

"Hey there," Ryan greeted his younger brother. "We don't do this often enough. And before you tell me all I do is work, I know it. You just have to shake me loose." Hugging his brother, Ryan signaled the bartender. "I'll have the same." As he looked at Tyler, he said, "You look like you haven't slept in a month. What's wrong? How can I help? Nothing's wrong with Sally?"

"Ah. There is definitely nothing wrong with my wife. It's me. I made Sally a promise I don't know how to keep."

"I'll need a little bit more if you want my advice," Ryan said as he sipped his scotch.

"First, I'm doing well at work. But the divorce cost me everything I'd saved, including a good chunk of my personal investments."

"I remember asking if you couldn't work something out with Victoria, and you said, 'You means short of killing her?'"

"To be free of that woman, I set up an annuity to pay her child support until Judy and Billy reached eighteen. I placed the house in her name and paid off the mortgage. And then bought a house for Sally and me to begin our life together."

"And even with your six figure salary, you're broke," Ryan commented, knowing full well that even his brother's retirement accounts had been signed over to his children.

"Oh, one more little item. Because I worried what would happen to Sally if I had an accident and died, I took out a four million dollar life insurance policy."

"With your smoking, even if they sold you a policy, the premiums…"

"Yeah. Are a fortune. But I also looked at it as a forced savings plan for our retirement. Money that I never saw in my pay and Victoria couldn't touch."

"What does Sally think about all this?"

"She's a trooper. She can make the buffalo jump on a nickel. And I am living on my expense account. So far it's working out."

"But?"

"The house is almost finished. And as you have seen, Sally has done a fabulous job painting and fixing it up... on a shoestring. So I told her that I wanted to take her on a trip to anyplace she wanted. A belated honeymoon."

"Okay, that could run a couple of thousand."

"Nope. Where do you think she wants to go? A dream she has had since fourth grade?"

"Haven't a clue. I think I am beginning to see your problem. Money. Right?"

"Antarctica!" Tyler took a gulp of his scotch. "I just checked with a travel agent and a trip to Antarctica for two could run around forty thousand dollars."

"Is Sally expecting you home for dinner?" Ryan asked, and not waiting for an answer pulled out his phone. "Call her and tell her I needed to speak to you so I invited you to dinner."

"Okay."

Settled at a nearby steakhouse, Ryan ordered a bottle of wine. Nothing would be solved if they were drunk on scotch. "I love this restaurant. It's a favorite with clients. At home, I cook burgers. The kids prefer that to a good steak," Ryan said as he bit into his New York strip steak. Savoring the taste, he saw that Tyler had yet to begin eating. "Starving won't help. Remember, I'm buying. Eat."

Over coffee, with nothing decided, Ryan tried to get his brother to select another destination, without success. "I think I've got a plan. Listen," Tyler said as he began to discuss how he was paid a flat salary and commissions on every client he brought to the firm. "So I will tell Sally we can schedule the trip for next year, and if both of us work together we could begin to save for the trip."

"Does she actually know what you take home?" Ryan asked.

"Not really. I turn over bonus checks, and I will just have to travel more, take more prospective clients out for dinner. All of which Sally will hate because I will rarely be home."

"If Sally went back to work..." Ryan began.

Tyler sat up straight and with a deadly look, declared, "My wife isn't going to work. I am going to give her everything."

As he took measure of his defiant brother, Ryan, suggested quietly, "I can lend you some money. Not forty thousand. But maybe ten thousand."

Tyler looked at his brother with tears brimming, shaking his head no. "I love you for offering, but this is my dilemma. I will just have to figure it out. Promise you won't say anything to Sally. Promise."

"Of course not. But if you get stuck, my offer stands."

Chapter 7

The day started with a light drizzle. "Fall is almost here," Tyler said. They were at the breakfast nook and were not planning on going to the club. It was going to be a family day. Listening to music, Tyler reading a new thriller and Sally mixing a new lotion she swore would ease Tyler's arthritic shoulder.

"Sally, we have to talk," he began. "I've made a decision about our trip. Instead of this December, why not take it next Christmas. Or at least in December."

"But..." Sally began, her forehead tight with tension.

He held up his hand to stop her. Tyler knew what she was going to say and didn't want to be reminded that they couldn't afford Antarctica. "Listen, okay?"

Sally leaned against the kitchen counter and waited.

"I've figured out that if I worked really hard to sign new clients, I could make more in bonuses and maybe even get a promotion with an increase in salary."

"But..."

"Sally, please listen to the rest. It requires your participation as well. And I wouldn't ask this of you, but it would enable you to have your dream."

She replenished his coffee and joined him at the table. Noticing the ashtray with a cigarette almost burned to ash she wrinkled her nose, looked at her stressed husband, and waited.

"In order to devote full time to signing new clients, I won't be able to do the club's books. I am going to ask you to take that over along with your usual recording of the minutes."

"Well that's more interesting than painting another room," she said with a slight smile, waiting for the other shoe to drop. Tyler was never this serious when he asked her to help him with any of his work-related plans. It was usually a spur of the moment, 'if you have time and would like to' kind of conversation.

"I am going to be targeting larger clients, ones that can afford larger retainers, and any proposal I prepare has to be perfect. Fortune 500 caliber. You were the best at this particular task of anyone I have ever worked with."

Sally thought of what her husband wasn't saying. It wasn't the work, she knew that while he was ambitious, he'd become driven. "Thank you, I think. Is there more?"

"I am afraid this isn't something you are going to like."

At that she got up and took down a couple of wine glasses. There was an open bottle of Malbec which she brought back to the table. "And?"

As Sally poured, Tyler reached for her hand and gently took the bottle. As he held that hand, he heaved a sigh. "And, to accomplish all this, it will require frequent dining with prospective clients and even more traveling than I have been doing."

"And I will be our here in Great Neck, all day and now most nights... alone," she said and took a long sip of her wine.

"Honeybunch. Do you hate me?"

Nodding no, she looked up into his deeply sad face. "You really want to do this? For a trip? Tyler, I can get a job," she cried.

"No wife of mine is going to work." Reaching over and cupping her chin in his fingers, he blew her a kiss. "Honeybunch. It's only for a year. Promise."

"But..."

"Actually, I want to do this for our future. This dream of yours is the first step. If I become the agency star in getting new business, our lives will be freed from constant worry about money. Wouldn't you like that?"

"Only if you promise on our love that this crazy schedule will stop on our return. I'm not Victoria. I don't need things. I need you," she cried as Tyler stood and pulled her into his arms. She was right. This was his angel. All she ever wanted was to be his wife.

Chapter 8

2018

Ryan had invited Sally and Tyler to dinner in the City the week before they were to leave for Antarctica. At Sally's suggestion he invited Jeanne to join them and celebrate their belated honeymoon trip. He had met Jeanne at the wedding five years before, but never really got a chance to know her.

As the four settled at the table in Ryan's favorite Italian restaurant, he opened the conversation. "You two have gone through so much, what with totally decorating and turning an empty house into a home and earning your potential promotion due to all the clients you managed to bring to the agency this year, I can only tell you both that I'm in awe. I not only love you but admire your teamwork when facing a challenge." As he picked up his wine glass, he said, "To Sally and Tyler. The best family this man could ever have."

"And, I have a present for Sally," said Jeanne. Handing over a dress size box wrapped in silver paper with a white lace bow, she saw the happy girl she knew as her former roommate, all smiles, as she reached out for the gift.

"Jeanne you shouldn't have. But I can't wait to see what you bought." Sally carefully unwrapped the package and pulled out a pale pink nightgown made in a light fleece fabric. "Oh Jeanne, if it weren't for the fabric it could be an evening gown," she gushed.

"And what did you bring for me?" Tyler teased.

Laughing, Jeanne said, "Sally in that nightgown." At that the group broke out in laughter.

"While we're giving presents," Ryan said, "Here, brother of mine, is one for you."

The surprise showed on Tyler's face as the brothers never exchanged gifts. Opening the wrapping paper he saw a digital camera he had been looking at for the past year. "How did you know?"

"Because that camera you showed me will never do justice to the magic of the trip you and my sister-in-law are taking. And, selfishly, I expect Sally to make a scrapbook for Jane and Mark to rival the *National Geographic*.

Chapter 9

The sounds of cutlery clinking against china permeated the room. Voices animated in conversation swirled around Sally and Tyler as they entered the dining room and headed to a table for two. It was their second night aboard ship of their celebratory cruise to the Antarctica Archipelago. Tonight they were looking forward to enjoying dinner now that their stomachs had finally settled.

The evening before, their first night aboard, the boat pitched and rolled on its rocky journey through the famed Drake's Passage, a body of water that has frightened seasoned seamen down through the centuries.

Today broke with bright sunshine and they had traveled ashore visiting colonies of penguins and later, sighting feeding whales from the deck of the ship. Tyler had been off aiming his new camera for one perfect photo after another, leaving Sally to mingle with other passengers, most of whom had made similar trips to other parts of the world.

Tonight, all smiles, Sally wore Tyler's favorite cocktail dress with a low back that allowed his hand to caress her bare skin. A heavenly shade of pink chiffon, the designer dress had nary a crease or wrinkle to mar her appearance. As they settled into their chairs, their waiter approached with a bottle of red wine.

"I can't believe that after one meal, Juan knows our favorite wine," Sally said, enjoying having her husband all to herself.

"It's their job to know our preferences, dear," he said and proceeded to order their dinner. Tyler looked at Sally with a wicked gleam in his eyes. "Did I tell you how lovely you look tonight?"

Sally blushed, becoming a shade of pink, setting off her blonde curls. She knew she was attractive, but when he looked at her like that she felt beautiful.

After clinking glasses and toasting to their love, Tyler set his glass down. "Out with it. There's something on your mind. You don't usually finger your silverware."

"Kind of. I've been worried about your smoking. There was an article in an online medical report that scared me to death. That in addition to the physical toll smoking takes on your lungs, cigarettes offer cancer other opportunities to attack your mouth, throat, tongue. And I don't know what else."

Tyler squeezed her hand in a gesture that was meant to calm her. "Honeybunch, you know I practically gave up smoking when we got married. It's just the stress of this past year that had me start again. I guess I never thought about how much I was smoking."

He was so handsome, she thought, for a moment forgetting her concerns. She fingered her salad fork and refocused her fears. "But now you smoke three packs, that's sixty cancer sticks every day. We've only been at sea one day and you're already edgy."

"Calm down," Tyler scolded. "The people at the next two tables are staring at us. You don't want the crew to know that I sneaked a cigarette on the back deck when it's clearly forbidden to smoke aboard ship."

"I love you so much, I don't want to lose you," she said, her voice rising in frustration.

"Quiet! You're making a scene," Tyler scolded, then turned and smiled at the couple at the next table. "My wife is worried about my health," he explained, all of his charm in full force.

What's wrong with him? Am I an embarrassment? In all their six years together, Tyler had never snapped at her. Not even when she was his executive assistant at the agency.

Apparently Tyler had appeased the adjacent table of diners, and in a lower voice she tried again. "Sweetheart, this is serious. Tell me the truth. Are the nicotine patches working?"

"Shush. And to answer your question, one patch a day isn't enough. I guess I'm using two a day. What does work is that tonic you packed. What's in it?"

"When I learned you couldn't smoke aboard, I checked my homeopathic references for something to keep you from nicotine withdrawal. The tonic contains tobacco added to water and boiled down into a thick liquid. For the past two days, I've been adding the syrup to your morning coffee. Just a little. It can be dangerous. You do know nicotine is a poison."

"Enough. Let's enjoy our dinner," Tyler said looking at his plate.

Dinner looked delicious, but as Sally began to eat her thoughts turned to the state of their marriage. This was supposed to be the honeymoon they never had. And here was her husband, not taking her concerns seriously, and now ignoring her to look over the other diners. This wasn't like him. He was normally so very attentive.

"Tyler, later, could we go into the lounge and have an after dinner drink? Enjoy ourselves a bit before we retire," Sally said hoping to restore their earlier happier mood.

"Honeybunch, what a wonderful idea. Especially about retiring to our cabin."

Oh yes, she sighed, and made a mental note not to bring up his smoking while on vacation.

The lounge was partially filled with passengers scattered among the room's sofas and tables. She noticed that most of the guests were couples and gathered in groups of four or six.

"Why don't you get us a table over there by the window and I'll get glasses of Prosecco to celebrate," Tyler said.

"Oh yes. Heavenly." Her ruse to get Tyler's attention had worked.

Patricia E. Gitt

As she sat at a window table, watching the passing scene of large ice flows and snow-capped outcrops of land, Sally noted that with twenty-three hours of daylight the full majesty of this end of the world had transformed at night into a panorama painted in hues of gray.

"May I join you," said a middle aged man Sally hadn't noticed before. "My name is Barry, and I saw you sitting by yourself. I'm traveling alone as well."

"She's not alone," was Tyler's curt remark. He leaned over Sally and handed her a glass of wine, whispering, "And what has you smiling?"

Sally turned and said, "You're jealous. You do know I adore you."

"Well, looking as delicious as you look, and knowing you as I do, yes Honeybunch, I admit it," he murmured into her ear.

"Barry – I'm Tyler and this lovely lady is my wife, Sally."

"You are a lucky man, Tyler. I'm sorry, I thought your wife was by herself. May I still join you? I'm a writer for a travel guide and here on assignment."

"Yes, please do. It was an honest mistake. If I'd seen Sally all by herself, I would certainly have introduced myself."

Sally smiled, knowing that wasn't too far from the truth. From the first day they'd met their attraction had been instantaneous. Now, some seven years later, here they were celebrating their sixth wedding anniversary.

40

Sally had dreamed of this trip as far back as high school and primed Tyler with information on everything from the animals they would encounter to why the ice flows they had seen were aqua, not white. And while not actually at the South Pole, they were still at the bottom of the world.

At first, the men had included her in their conversation. Barry filled them in on the next day's excursion where he hoped to photograph the penguins feeding, possibly spot whales circling in a pod to feed, and seals sunning on the stretches of ice and snow. Then talk turned to topics that excluded her. She was sure it wasn't by design. It was just a men's thing. All she could do was watch the two men chat about golf, baseball... they were both Yankee fans, and maybe later finding partners for a game of poker.

"Tyler, Sally, it's been a delight. Thank you for sharing your time with this solo traveler," Barry said as he rose to leave. "What a coincidence, all from New York City. When this trip is over maybe we can get together and share photos," he offered.

Sally watched Barry walk to the bar, and smiling, with hope in every word, asked Tyler, "Are we ready to turn in?"

"Not yet," was Tyler's quick reply. "I never thought I'd meet such an interesting group of people. From what I've seen their conversation is above average and more worldly than I had expected. Let's go over to that table and introduce ourselves. They look like they are having fun."

Tyler was in his meet and greet, and let's get together when we get back to the States, mode. All she could do was play the compliant wife.

Later, when the door of their cabin closed, Sally could no longer hold her anger. "You're killing yourself with cigarettes. As if that isn't enough, you're never home but traveling on business, leaving me to fester in suburbia. Then when you are home you continue schmoozing at the country club while I'm shunted off with the wives... and all they talk about is their children. Children, may I remind you, that we don't have. The most important thing to me is having a family. But no, you won't even go to a doctor to find out why we haven't gotten pregnant."

Tyler sat stunned at Sally's outburst. "Honeybunch, stop! I had no idea you were unhappy. I've never seen you so... upset. Not once in all the years we've been together."

Sally realized that she had dumped all her anger on the one person she loved above all others. "Tyler, it isn't that I'm unhappy, just frustrated. The house is ready. I'm ready. This trip was to celebrate our love. Bring us back to those early days before I tore the house apart to paint every nook and cranny. I can finally wear makeup, set my hair and wear filmy dresses like before we married. I was looking forward to this trip with tender dinners and sweet coupling. So far, all you seem to be doing is looking for business contacts. What's happened to us?"

Feeling Tyler's arms and his body's familiar reaction to being close, she stiffened. "Now you want to make love?" Pushing away and burying her head in a pillow, Sally's sobs permeated the small cabin.

"Honeybunch. I always want to make love to you," Tyler whispered as he sat on the edge of the bed and stroked her back.

"Well I have a headache," she said and the sobs continued. Even though she knew he hadn't moved, she could feel him withdraw, his hand no longer on her back. Reaching out to pull him close, she knew her anger was simple frustration, she loved this man more every day. "Kiss me, and forget my bad mood," she whispered. "We have all night to make up."

Chapter 10

He couldn't wait to get back to the cabin. Barry could never compose a lengthy email on his cell, his stubby fingers kept hitting the wrong letters. When on assignment he always used a laptop. After a quick pit stop and running a comb through his almost non-existent hair, Barry picked up the machine and headed for the lounge bar. A drink to celebrate one-upping his brother, the callous Warren, who would owe him royally with this bit of news.

To: Warren Lazar

From: Barry Lazar

Subject: Surprise!

Greetings Big Brother – Do I have a tidbit for you. My magazine has sent me on a tourist expedition to Antarctica. And your tropical loving younger brother is suffering daily, bundled up in four layers of clothes, sunglasses and thermal gloves. Boy, what I have to do to make a living. Not like you and your easy-peasy executive position at that agency. Heat in winter, air conditioning in summer and an office all your own looking out over the Hudson River.

Well, dear brother, it's my second night aboard the ship and I was eating dinner. Who do I see across the dining room, but Tyler Scott, your competition. He and a young cutie pie were having an intense conversation.

Well, that's it. I guess it's past your bedtime in New York, or almost breakfast. I can't keep these time zones straight.

Bye,

Barry

Almost asleep, Barry heard his computer's incessant buzzing. Who in hell was contacting him at this time of night. Struggling out from under his cocoon of blankets, he took a step, groaning as he stubbed a toe on his suitcase pushed off to the side of the bed. On opening his computer he saw the icon for incoming email.

"It'll just have to wait." About to tuck back under the blankets, he now had to take a trip to the bathroom, only to find on returning the renewed racket of incoming mail. "Shit! I cleared it. Now what?"

This time he opened the link and a quick glance saw that his brother had sent him four emails. The local time aboard was 12:30 am.

It couldn't have been more than one hour since I sent him my news. What does he want from me? Probably my hide. When will I learn not to do him any favors. I always get cussed out for them.

11:33 PM

To: Barry

From: Warren

Subject: Critical…

Okay here's what you are going to do. You are going to shadow the bastard and listen for anything I can use to cause him trouble at the office. Anything. Got it."

11:36 PM

To: Barry

From: Warren

Subject: Don't fail me.

The prick is up for the same promotion I am. I want it. Who is he with? He's supposed to be on vacation with his wife. But I know he's sneaking off for nooners with his secretary and she wasn't in today.

11:39 PM

To: Barry

From: Warren

Subject: What the hell are you doing when I'm trying to reach you?

Call me. Now!!!

11:44 PM

To: Barry

From: Warren

Subject: Fuck it! Get back to me immediately!

I don't care if it costs you a week's salary. In your case probably two weeks. Phone, don't email.

It had been Barry's practice when on an assignment to disconnect from the office. He had no children and no contact with his former wife for six years. Warren was his only family. Since he never called out of brotherly love, Barry saw no reason to keep his cell on, preferring to use it when it was convenient for him, not the caller. But the laptop was a tool, part computer, part phone and part photoshop. A necessity when developing an article, especially one about this expedition where the pictures would tell most of the story. Unlike his phone, it was always on, even when being charged.

Grumpy didn't quite explain his bleak mood as he pulled on his pants, threw on a large bulky sweater and headed to the main reception area. He wasn't even sure he could place a call from the middle of the ice bordered channel. "Hell, we're heading towards the South Pole, not Buenos Aires and civilization."

"Yes, Mr. Lazar. How may I help you?" the very efficient uniformed young man asked.

"Is there any way I can make a phone call to New York City?"

Patricia E. Gitt

"Yes, but I must tell you that would be very expensive. Can't you send an email? It would be far cheaper. You can use our computer if you don't have one."

If I don't have one? Who in this day and age wasn't connected? "Unfortunately, I need to make a call. It's an emergency. I'll be quick."

The steward looked the man over and saw he was overweight of medium height, bleary-eyed and disheveled. It was hard not to notice that he had forgotten to zip his pants. Since he was empowered to let passengers use their main phone connection to the continent for emergencies, he was guessing this was one of those occasions. "Step this way, Mr. Lazar. You will have to limit your time to no more than four minutes."

As he entered the back office, Barry nodded his understanding.

The steward settled at an electronic console and asked, "May I have the phone number?"

As Barry gave the young man Warren's home number, he wondered why his normally self-involved brother who rarely gave him a minute's attention was demanding he call.

The young man checked the connection with a local operator, read him the phone number then handed the handset to Barry.

"What in hell were you doing? Why can't you ever do anything I ask? Is a phone call beyond your skill set?" greeted Barry before he'd had a chance to say hello.

48

"Warren, for Christ's sake. What has you so riled up? I'm in the middle of an ice-bound channel, not in a luxury hotel with a phone on my bedside table."

"Riled up? You know how I hate Tyler Scott. Your little tidbit could insure my promotion to Executive Vice President, imbecile. Just because your editor sends you on a holiday doesn't mean you can ignore me. Remember, without me you'd be on the street. You owe me."

"What do you want this time? Blood?" Barry should never have sent that email. Now his mercenary brother would hound him for the rest of the trip demanding more and more. Of what he wasn't sure. It wasn't as if Tyler Scott was the only man Warren was out to destroy. But it was just his luck that the man on the top of that list was on the same ship.

"Listen carefully. I want you to send me a photo of the woman he's with. I want you to listen in on his conversations. Bring his name up with other passengers. I want you to find something I can hang him with. Got it! Buy him drinks. Make him confide in you."

A nudge by the steward reminded Barry his time was up. "Okay. Don't yell. I'm not alone, and I don't want to fight. But I'm not your lackey. And if you calm down you will realize I'm working. I'm not spying for the illustrious Warren Lazar."

"Sir, I have to disconnect the line," the steward said, interrupting Barry as quietly as he could.

"Have to hang up. I'll email anything I learn. But don't expect me to poison his dinner for you. You can do that yourself."

Barry stood in place, not knowing where he was going to go next. Bed? He wasn't going to get any sleep now. The steward had disconnected the communications link and looked like he'd wished he not heard Barry's end of the conversation.

"Thank you, young man. I appreciate your help with this family matter," he said and handed him a US twenty dollar bill.

"We rarely connect our passengers to a mainland line. I am just glad to have helped you out."

"Ah, could you tell me if there is a bar open at this hour?"

"The one just outside the dining hall may still be open. If not you can call room service. Good night, Mr. Lazar."

Room service. Right. And with the drink almost in hand, he stumbled his way back to his cabin.

Chapter 11

Liam heard the screech. Instinct and five years as a guide on Antarctic expeditions told him it wasn't a chinstrap penguin calling to his mate. It had to be a human in distress. Surveying the surrounding snow-covered landscape, his eyes fell on a figure in the distance wrapped in a brightly colored orange parker, kneeling on the snow.

"Mrs. Scott," he said softly as he approached the clearly unhinged woman rocking back and forth on her knees. Her running eyes and nose transformed what he knew to be a pretty face. Liam gently lifted Sally Scott to her feet and tried to see if she was just crying or in some sort of pain. "What's wrong?" The devastated look she turned towards him was followed by her pointing down into a crevasse of deep aqua blue tinted snow.

Oh my God. In all ten years of his experience as an expedition guide he'd never had a tourist die on his watch. Yet, he knew from the angle of the head as the body lay crumpled at the bottom of the ten-foot crack in the compacted snow, this woman's husband was almost certainly dead.

"Mrs. Scott, stay with me while I get help. The ship's doctor can be with us in minutes." Trained for incidents of this kind, Liam called the captain on his radio and told him of Mr. Scott's fall, requesting assistance to bring him up to the surface, and alert the doctor to what he would face as the ship's medical officer. He was careful not to add to Mrs. Scott's distress by telling the captain that he thought the man was already dead.

Assured that the ship's emergency team would be out shortly, Liam returned his attention to the rest of the expedition's passengers wandering a little distance away, over the snow-covered terrain.

Liam knew it wasn't unusual for Mr. Scott to have wandered away from the landing party. Gently moving Mrs. Scott away from the edge of the yawning opening in the snow, Liam waved to one of the other guides and holding his handset, waited for the five other guides to get on their radios.

"Would you keep everyone away from this area? I've called for the ship's rescue team. There has been an accident."

The hand-held radio crackled with the question he dreaded. Turning away from the hysterical woman, he replied, "Carlos, it's Mr. Scott. We won't know any more until we reach him and check for a pulse."

Liam, never leaving Sally out of his sight, began to question the circumstances that led to this tragic accident. He hoped for her sake it was simply that, an accident. If there was even a hint of foul play, Argentina would wrap the entire ship in red tape while they prosecuted the death.

* * *

The cabin on the Explorer was spacious but not large enough to pace away her grief. Just remembering the doctor's kind offer of assistance brought a new flood of tears. While her husband lay dead on the examination table, Doctor Bob had been explaining each step of his methodical examination of Tyler's broken body. All Sally could think about was having promised Tyler before they left on their cruise that if he was injured and couldn't live an active life she wouldn't take extraordinary measures to keep him alive. Tyler had been proud of his carefully toned physique and she knew he would have preferred death to living as a cripple.

Her sobbing began again, as she remembered that conversation and Tyler's response. "Sweetheart, how can you even think of dying? We are going on vacation. A belated honeymoon." As she blew her now sore nose, Sally remembered her reply. " We've never discussed it before. This voyage could be dangerous and it seemed reasonable to have this chat."

Refocusing on Dr. Bob's information, she learned that the ship would continue on its journey down the Antarctica Archipelago and be back in Ushuaia in three days. "So, you see Mrs. Scott, the waterline is below freezing, allowing us to keep your husband's body safe until we return to port."

Now, alone in her cabin, Sally couldn't keep her mind off the shattering sound of Tyler's scream. Why hadn't she stayed by his side? She was close enough to keep him from falling. But he never paid attention to anyone's rules when they got in the way of a great photo. It was something she had gotten accustomed to. But how did he slip? Her husband was a weekend athlete, sure footed, energetic and as balanced as one of his beloved golf clubs... unless of course he'd been drinking. And he'd had several scotches the evening before while sharing sports stories with that reporter.

As she looked around the cabin she revisited the emotional roller coaster of the evening before. Sally never had reason to shout or complain about anything. Tyler was always so considerate, loving, supportive. The walls of the cabin offering no solace, she realized that her frustration had been building for months. One disappointment after another, beginning at dinner. Tyler not wanting to discuss his smoking, his curt demands she not make a scene, then ignoring her in the lounge after dinner. It had all come rushing out. Overwrought, she had even turned away from Tyler in bed, until having calmed down she reached out and gave him a deep, love filled kiss that led to their passionate lovemaking that was as natural as breathing.

Shocked by the memory she cringed from a deep, soul pain. *Oh, if I could only live that evening over.* Mortification at her anger and the last words she'd spewed at the love of her life rendered her numb, and collapsing on the floor, she was impervious to the gently rocking ship. *I should have kept my frustrations to myself.*

Chapter 12

It was the morning of the last day of the cruise and the ship was docked back in Ushuaia. Sally was to meet the captain in the dining room after breakfast. All other passengers had since disembarked for their journeys home.

Still numb but braced for the ordeal ahead, Sally was comforted by the kindness of the crew who had never left her side. The captain, the doctor, or Liam were always nearby, even joining her for meals.

Now she was about to begin the journey of widowhood. In the two days following Tyler's accident she had been consumed by the everyday details of life aboard ship. Passengers she and Tyler had met often stopped by to chat, some inviting her to join them for trips ashore. She'd accepted, hoping that the magic of Antarctic wildlife would ignite a spark of life she'd need to go forward.

All packed, she stood in navy traveling clothes, wishing they were black. A new day, another hurdle, she thought. On entering the salon, Sally saw a slim, severely suited older man standing alongside the captain and Liam.

"Mrs. Scott, may I introduce Alejandro Diaz. Senor Diaz is an attorney and was hired by the company to help you navigate the Argentine legal system. Before you can leave Ushuaia, or Argentina, the government must rule on your husband's death. We are sorry that practical matters must be discussed before you disembark the ship."

Sally appreciated once again the sensitivity of the captain, his soothing way of communicating additional details of her situation. While she was the widow, he represented the ship's owners.

"Mrs. Scott," Senior Diaz began in excellent, slightly accented English, "Doctor Marshall and Liam Sanford have compiled a thorough record of the accident and examination of your husband's body, both at the scene and later in the doctor's office aboard ship. They have provided me with notarized reports along with photographs of the scene and the body of your husband prior to the doctor's examination to determine a cause of death."

"But it was an accident," Sally cried in confusion. Looking over to Liam, she cried, "I should have gone with him. I could have reached out and helped him regain balance."

"Mrs. Scott, I was there. There wasn't anything you could have done. In fact, if you had reached out to hold your husband, he could have pulled you with him."

"Mrs. Scott," Captain Larson said as he filled her cup with tea, "my company is devastated by your loss. In all the forty years at sea, I've never encountered an accident of this kind. As a company we take every precaution to ensure the safety of our passengers, and I might add, that of our crew. I want to assure you that we will take care of you throughout this entire process. In fact, your husband's body was just picked up by the Ushuaia authorities and taken to the morgue."

All she could think of was the costs involved in staying in this remote community. Hotels, meals, airline rebooking fees along with any unexpected incidentals. "Gentlemen, I can't afford to stay here for more than a day or two. Won't it take weeks to sort this out?"

Sally watched in surprise as Liam spoke for the first time during their meeting. "Mrs. Scott, I will be accompanying you during this process, no matter how long it takes. And I assure you that any costs involved will be taken care of by the company."

* * *

She had been in a pleasant hotel for the past five days, hardly aware of her surroundings in this make-believe end-of-the-world setting.

"...and the Judge has agreed to accept our reports of your husband's death as an accident," Senor Diaz reported. "It will take some time for the autopsy to be completed, but initial findings have enabled them to give a final ruling on your husband's death."

"Autopsy?" Trying not to show her fright, Sally wondered if the extra nicotine patches, and her doubling her potion on the morning of the accident would be discovered during the autopsy. Was she responsible for Tyler's fall?

"I'm sorry. Did you say that the ruling was that Tyler's death was an accident? She felt hollow, weary. "Senor Diaz, does this mean this is over and I can go home?"

"Si, Senora."

"Can I have my husband's body cremated and take him home with me?" At that moment, the mere thought of the thousands of dollars it might cost to ship Tyler's body home for burial scared her more than what any autopsy report might say.

"Yes, the judge has requested the morgue release the body and I can contact a funeral home to arrange for cremation."

"Then I can contact the airlines for reservations?" While hopeful of leaving that day and putting the entire tragedy behind her, Sally knew she would be here at least another couple of days.

"Mrs. Scott. Please let me take care of your reservations from Ushuaia to Buenos Aires and on to New York," Liam said as he looked to the kindly attorney. "Alejandro, will it be possible for Mrs. Scott to leave the day after tomorrow?"

"Most certainly, Liam. Mrs. Scott, please accept my invitation to dinner tonight. My way to express my sympathy for the end of what has to have been a terrible ordeal."

"Thank you, Mr. Diaz. I can't vouch for my mood but appreciate your kind invitation. It would be a nice way to end this tragic affair. A social evening, instead of another formal meeting with government officials. Maybe Liam can join us. I wish Captain Larsen were here. But I understand he had to depart on another cruise. It means a lot to me that you were both with me every step of the way."

Chapter 13

Sally tipped the bellman, placing her bags at the front desk of the Ushuaia hotel. Liam phoned earlier to tell her he would pick her up at ten and accompany her to the airport for the trip home. He had become a trusted friend, always there to answer questions, and staying by her side throughout the ten day ordeal of lawyers and government officials assisting in finalizing the details surrounding Tyler's death. Now he would see that she passed through customs swiftly with all necessary paperwork in order.

With a sigh, Sally wandered out of the hotel. She wanted one last look at this town at the end of Argentina that drew travelers from all over the world.

Ushuaia harbor was a postcard picture of a sleepy community. Founded in 1884 as an outpost to the British Empire and now part of Argentina, its motto is *Ushuaia, end of the world, beginning of everything.*

The town itself was built on a slope down to the harbor. The older buildings reminded her of Bermuda some forty years before with its one and two-story wood framed shops.

As she reached the edge of the Beagle Channel, the gateway to the Antarctica Archipelago, Sally gazed out to the water before her. The mountain range on the left was in Chile, and the peaks of Argentina's mountains lay behind her. Ushuaia was literally at the end of the continent, capped by its famous Tierra del Fuego National Park, which attracted hikers and visitors seeking the undeveloped beauty of nature.

Sally, now seated in her business class seat for the last leg of her trip home, had explored its flexible flatbed design and the buttons for angling it to fit her level of comfort. Next she checked the monitor for selections of movies, television and musical offerings. It was more out of nerves than planning her selection. Finally, a bit calmer, she sat back and silently thanked the cruise company for this added gift, this cocoon of privacy that was nothing like the cramped seating she and Tyler had shared on the trip out.

Sipping a martini that the steward had placed on a shelf at her side, Sally waited for dinner service to begin, allowing her thoughts to roam. Who was this woman, traveling alone? Some wealthy person of privilege? Then tears began to form. No, she was a widow, alone with her grief.

As her drink began to work its soothing magic, Sally knew that whatever lay ahead, she wasn't alone. Jeanne, along with warm and caring Ryan, would help her through the days ahead.

Buck up. Stop whining, Sally Compton Scott. Sitting up, she decided she was going to enjoy every moment of the eleven-hour flight with its drinks, food and comfort.

Chapter 14

Ryan was devastated by Sally's call from the ship with news that the brother he had raised like a son was dead. "Oh Sally, we loved him so much," he whispered. It was almost midnight and with the kids asleep upstairs, he was alone with his grief.

Closing his eyes, Ryan thought back to those grade school years where he tried to instill confidence in the growing young man. After their parents had died in a car crash, Ryan, only eight years older, had been father, sole support and best friend to a boy who always felt inferior to his schoolmates. While he had worked hard to provide a safe life for them both, there was little spare time for his brother. But he knew that Tyler was aware that while they were safe with a roof over their heads, money was an everyday problem. "Oh and you did pitch in," Ryan said, as he remembered the ten year old delivering local newspapers before school. "I guess we were more roommates than family."

I have to be strong for Sally. She needs me now. Sally, you are more a Scott than any of us, he thought. *You are an angel in disposition, smart, and a full partner in my brother's marriage.*

"She must be beyond grief. Sally loved Tyler above all else. She made him finally feel safe. If I didn't love her for herself, I would have loved her for that." He sighed. *You gave my brother a sense of self-worth and a maturity I never could.*

It had been a night of tossing and turning, his sheets now a tangle around his legs. Ryan's thoughts turned to Tyler's life of constant striving for some unattainable goal. Ryan had gone through a similar phase trying to figure out if, at eighteen, he was strong enough to raise his younger brother. But over the years he had come to terms with his short-comings. Tyler never did. It wasn't just money that had been the driving force behind his brother's devotion to his career. What drove his brother since he met Sally was simply that he wanted to be the best of husbands. Tyler knew the costs of a bad marriage and it was more than dollars.

Ryan had been there to help counsel the ambitious young man. All was well with the Scott boys until Tyler married his first wife, Victoria.

A picture of Tyler and Victoria at their wedding flashed in view. "Oh why, why did you ever marry that woman?" he cried, the strength of the sound jarring him awake.

"Thank God for Sally, she saved your life."

Chapter 15

"Yeah, yeah, Warren. The widow is on her way back to New York."

Barry had waited until he returned home before calling his brother about the tragic death of Tyler Scott. While details hadn't been shared with the passengers, the captain, joining passengers gathered for a pre dinner drink in the lounge, had made an announcement, simply saying that Mr. Scott had died in a fall during the morning's landing. That due to the ongoing investigation no details were available. He hoped they would be sensitive to Mrs. Scott's grief and not communicate the tragedy to people outside the ship.

Barry had liked Sally Scott and was only too willing to respect her privacy. She had kept to her cabin, but one morning he brought her a cup of coffee and personally offered his condolences. It was the least he could do.

Tired of being his brother's servant, Barry relegated him to that closed place in his mind, where Warren didn't exist. It was the only way to prevent him from ruining the balance of the trip. News of Tyler Scott's demise could wait. So for the balance of the trip he had enjoyed the wonders of nature along with the other passengers, capturing photos and recording reactions of passengers and crew for his upcoming feature.

"Well, well, Barry old boy, this news couldn't have come at a more convenient time. Gotta run. Have to gather the bastard's files before the office knows he's dead."

* * *

It was after six and the offices of Brown, Delroy and Marcus were practically empty. As long as he didn't run across Mr. Brown, the founding partner who was somewhere in his eighties, Warren knew he'd be safe. *The man must sleep here,* he thought.

Entering Tyler Scott's office he first accessed his assistant's computer. "Yup. All nicely organized." Removing a flash drive from his jacket pocket, Warren set about copying each of Tyler's nine client files.

On second thought, did she also have a password keeper? That way I can access everything from my computer at home. "Yup! Good girl."

With one last look around the assistant's area, he quickly walked into the inner office and saw a room that would pass for a surgical suite in any hospital. Not a file, note, or pen in sight. *Well, well, another thing we don't have in common,* he thought and moved around to the desk. *I'm smart. You're not. I'm cutthroat. You're not. And you're dead.*

The first stop was behind the desk to open the main drawer. "No surprise here. It's locked." It didn't take long to know that all drawers were also locked tightly, and after checking he found all other cabinets were securely locked as well.

"Let me see. I've got access to his computer. I wonder what I can find to crucify your memory. Now I'm the only one in contention for promotion. Take that, you bastard."

With that Warren returned to his office, picked up his laptop and slipped the flash drive into his pocket, left for home and a stiff drink before going through Tyler Scott's files.

Chapter 16

"Mrs. Scott. My name is Leslie Ann Fields. I'm with the National American Insurance Company and hoped we might meet to discuss your late husband's insurance policy." She could tell by the silence at the other end of the phone her call was unexpected.

"Ms. Fields? I don't understand. I'm under a bit of pressure planning my husband's funeral and all."

She heard the soft tremulous voice of a woman in her late twenties. "Yes. I fully understand the strain you're under. If we could have a brief chat now that would help. I won't take long. I just need a bit of information before the company can begin to process your claim."

"Couldn't this wait until I bury my husband? I haven't been home long enough to get things sorted."

Did she hear a slight bristling? Was this a situation that required more than a simple verification of death? She hoped not. She had delayed a planned vacation to help Edwin Rothstein handle this client. "I am sorry to intrude. If now isn't convenient, I could call back tomorrow."

"Look here, Ms. Fields. Do you realize that I haven't slept in forty-eight hours? In fact, I'm still on Argentina time.

And, I've spent another week of sleepless nights before the government would allow me to leave Ushuaia. That's at the end of the world if you didn't know. Anyway, how did you get my number?"

"I'm so sorry, Mrs. Scott. Your attorney contacted our office to let us know of your husband's death. He gave me permission to call you. Most of my questions can wait until after we receive the autopsy results. I just need to check on a couple of details about your trip to Antarctica. I am afraid that can't wait if you want your husband's four million dollar policy to be paid in a timely manner."

"Autopsy?"

"I will need a copy of the autopsy report from the Argentinian authorities in Ushuaia. It's the company's normal procedure in deaths of this kind." Leslie heard a quick intake of breath. "Mrs. Scott, are you all right?"

"No. No. It was an accident," was the strangled reply. "The Argentine authorities ruled death by accidental fall... that I was free to cremate Tyler's remains for easier transport home."

"About that. I am afraid for any claim to be processed, especially one of this size, the company requires a copy of an official autopsy report."

"Ms. Fields..."

"Leslie, please."

"Maybe you could enlighten me. Just what does National American Insurance require of me? As if an official certificate of my husband's death isn't enough to complete your paperwork. Maybe an invitation to his funeral would satisfy your requirements."

"Sarcasm won't solve anything, Mrs. Scott. I can assure you I do not want to cause you any further stress." *Well, well, Edwin was right. This case may call on my experience as a profiler with the police department. Something in her reaction just isn't adding up. And won't Edwin be happy if the death wasn't accidental.*

"Just give me your number and I will get in touch tomorrow. I still have to call the funeral home and Tyler's boss. I don't even know where Tyler kept a copy of the policy," Sally all but snapped.

"Of course. But no need to call me. I'll get back in a day or two. Goodbye, Mrs. Scott, and please accept my sincerest sympathies for your loss." Leslie hung up before she could hear another excuse as to why the woman wouldn't take the time to answer a couple of questions over the phone. If the widow hadn't initially sounded fragile, she might have taken her evasion as a sign of possible misconduct. Leslie knew her job was to continue investigating the death. National American Insurance wasn't going to release payment of four million dollars until she had turned over every rock. So far, the only information she had was the shipping manifest confirming delivery of the ashes to the funeral parlor, Sampson & Sons, in New Jersey.

* * *

"Edwin, you may be right to look into Scott's death. Ah dinnae ken," Leslie said as she sat facing the president of the insurance company to discuss next steps.

69

Patricia E. Gitt

"Dinnae ken?" Edwin repeated.

"Aye. I don't know," Leslie replied. She tried not to use her Scottish expressions, knowing that her boss had no patience for conversation over and above the nuts and bolts of a case. They were in the New York City office of the National American Insurance Company, a place Leslie rarely visited since her official retirement three years before. Since then, when Edwin needed an expert witness or someone who could finagle information from a policy holder, he hired her on a freelance basis. It was an arrangement Leslie liked. Now she had time in the spring and summer to tend her garden and enjoy off season travel during the fall and winter months.

"I'm depending upon the skeptical Scot in you to prove this death wasn't an accident. Apparently you picked something up during your brief conversation with the widow."

Edwin was a man in his late fifties and she had worked with him for the past twenty years. Leslie knew he relied on her ability to sniff out potential evasions by claimants.

"I know you planned a vacation… and I would have put another investigator on this case," he continued, "but the location alone, being off the beaten path and relatively inaccessible was unusual. And this is a younger, second wife. Usually there's a story there as well. Now you are telling me that you think the widow may be hiding something." Edwin couldn't hide his interest.

"Just a feeling, something isn't right." Leslie's thick Scottish accent was heavy as she tried to capture that something that had set her antennae on alert. "Sorry, but she has me curious about this entire matter."

"Women," Edwin said. "You are much better at getting behind someone's scheming ways than any male investigator I might assign to clear this claim," he stated in his no nonsense way.

"Scheming ways? How antediluvian of you. Next you are going to tell me that I inherited some witchlike ways from my Celtic ancestors. That my training in psychology has nothing to do with my skill in profiling people."

"Don't get your Scottish temper up. I was trying to pay you a compliment."

"I dinna get my temper up. It's just that somehow her reaction didn't ring completely true. Yes, his death was probably traumatic. And, yes, she knows he had a policy. Edwin, she wasn't surprised by the amount. But she was evasive about setting a day or time to meet with me."

"Okay," Edwin said as he pulled out the Tyler Scott file. "I'm counting on your ability to find anything that might suggest the accident had help. One more little item. Mrs. Tyler Scott, the first wife, called, wanting to know when she would receive her portion of the policy."

"Och, two wee widows. Another wrinkle," Leslie said as she gathered the file and her tote bag and left Edwin to his paperwork.

.

Chapter 17

"Jeanne, I'm so glad you're home. Can I stop up? I'm in the city." Sally was unaware that her pleading tone carried over the noise in the Pennsylvania train station.

Jeanne had kept the secret of her double life, that while working for Tyler as his executive assistant at the agency they had been having a steamy affair. Whenever Tyler's wife held tough on the divorce Sally would cry out her misery to Jeanne. During many teary, wine-filled evenings, she'd share the harpy's increasing demands as Tyler's patience wore thin and finally capitulated, sinking into near bankruptcy to satisfy the demands of Victoria, his shrew of a wife.

"Of course. I just got home from work. I even have leftovers for dinner," was Jeanne's happy reply.

"Don't go out of the way for me. I just need your company and wise advice."

Jeanne warmly embraced Sally, leading her to the living room of the one-bedroom apartment. "Now sit, I'll pour you a glass of your favorite white wine."

With a sigh, Sally took off her raincoat and accepted the glass from her best friend in the whole world. "I needed to talk to someone... someone who knew about my marriage to Tyler."

Jeanne settled onto the sofa next to Sally. "After you introduced him to me I was jealous. I'd never seen two people so blissfully happy."

Happy. Until recently, Sally thought, and lifted her glass in a toast. "Here's to love and dreams, may they actually exist."

"That's a far cry from the Mrs. Tyler Scott I've known these past six years," Jeanne said, moving closer on the sofa. "I know you're grieving. Tyler's death has to be devastating. I received your email about next month's memorial service. Is that what you need my help for? You know I'll do anything I can to ease you through it."

"No. The funeral home is handling everything. I gave them a list of people to notify and they will be sending official announcements. I scheduled it for next month to give myself time to get my footing." As she sipped her wine, Sally finally admitted she couldn't face her predicament alone. She and Tyler were a team. She missed him, his love and guidance.

"I'm a wreck. Can't seem to make sense of anything. What am I going to do with my life? How am I going to pay for it? The monthly bills were waiting for me when I got home," Sally cried, wringing her hands. "When we married I stopped working. Without Tyler's salary, I barely have enough in my savings account to carry me three months. The truth is we lived pretty much paycheck to paycheck."

"Sally, you told me how happy you and Tyler were. What changed? The last time we spoke you had finished your year-long campaign to turn that new house into a showplace."

"Yeah... a showplace. I painted the entire interior, even made curtains. But the only two rooms that meant anything to me were our master bedroom and the soon to be nursery. Now I'll have to put it on the market," Sally said before taking another long sip of her wine.

"Sally, are you finally pregnant?" Jeanne's face lit up.

"I'm not pregnant," she said, the pain in her voice more poignant than her renewing tears. "I'm a widow without the family I dreamed of," she sobbed. "Living in a house mortgaged into the next century. I don't even know if Tyler's company will continue sending his bonus checks for clients he brought to the firm."

"That's a load of shit for anyone to deal with," Jeanne said, handing Sally a box of tissues. "Let's list things to do and place them in some timeline. It won't seem so overwhelming that way. Okay?"

As Sally fell back into the soft sofa, her tears turned to anger. "My first priority is dealing with Ms. Fields of the National American Insurance Company."

"Already? You haven't been home a week?"

The attorney called my insurance agent to tell him about Tyler's accident. I had hoped he would tell me what to do. You know, legally."

Sally's mind slowed. She was here, safe with Jeanne. Her best and only friend. "Can I have a refill?" Sally asked, reaching for the vodka instead of the wine. "I can't deal with Fields now. I told her I didn't even know where Tyler kept the policy."

"Calm down," Jeanne advised. "Breathe. That's right... in and out. Sally, is there something you aren't telling me? You seem too upset, not in the weepy just lost my husband way. Is it something deeper?"

Sally sat silently, shrinking into herself.

"Perhaps a dustup during your cruise?" Jeanne prompted.

"Sort of," Sally whispered as the tears cascaded down her pale face. "I had dreamed of this trip since I was a little girl. I wanted to experience walking on the white continent and seeing the penguins, seals, and whales up close." Dabbing at her eyes, she continued, "Tyler hates cold weather. I tried to get him excited about the trip, telling him that Antarctica was the location of the famed voyage Ernest Shackleton began in 1907. Tyler's somewhat of a history buff and that seemed to pique his interest. Unfortunately, my husband's ideal vacation was golfing in some hot climate," she cried clutching Jeanne's hand. "He took this trip for me. I was feeling lonely and unappreciated with his working longer hours and traveling more to sign new clients. It's my fault."

Jeanne moved closer on the sofa and enfolded Sally in a hug. But the embrace was short lived as Sally jumped up and began to pace the room.

"We should have gone to the Bahamas. It would have been far cheaper. Then maybe he wouldn't keep saying that we needed more money."

Patricia E. Gitt

"But he did enjoy the cruise?" Jeanne asked.

"Yeah. He loved mingling with the other passengers. It's just that the night before his accident we had a fight," she said, fingering her wedding ring. "I should have been all dreamy, wanting to make love. And for the first time in, well ever, I hit him with all my frustrations. Bang, bang, bang, one after another."

Jeanne's eyes widened. "What? Why? You've always told me that all you had to do was look at one another and you'd be tearing off your clothes. What got you so angry?"

Shit, just get it out. "I was furious about him ignoring me all evening. And I was worried about his sneaking out on deck for a cigarette when I wasn't looking. In fact, at one point he told me to shut up. Can you imagine?"

"Tyler? Were you with a large group of people?"

"No, worse. We were at a small table. But the neighboring tables heard every word. I could have jumped overboard. I was so embarrassed," Sally confessed, clenching the cocktail glass that was on the verge of shattering.

"And…"

"Well, you know me. Quiet as a mouse Sally. I kept it together, things got back to a sociable normal. But no sooner had we closed the door on our stateroom, I reached out and almost slapped Tyler so hard it would have left a red mark."

Jeanne got up and refilled her friend's empty glass, this time with more ice than vodka.

"Something in me must have snapped because for ten minutes I listed all the frustrations that had been building over the evenings and weekends he was off doing something or other, leaving me in that empty house. No car, no money and no real friends.

"The next morning I realized Tyler's unusual outburst was probably due to nicotine withdrawal. He's never embarrassed me or treated me as if I didn't matter."

As the sobbing resumed, Jeanne reached up and pulled Sally back to the sofa. "Of course, you made up."

"Yes. You know I can't be arm's length from Tyler without jumping his bones. And now I'm a widow," she sobbed.

"Why do you think his smoking was a problem?"

"Because the only time Tyler was ever sharp with me was when he couldn't smoke. And usually it was a fuss about something stupid."

Jeanne handed Sally another tissue. "What happened the next morning?"

"We'd made love and a couple of hours later he died."

"If you were back in each other's arms, nicotine deprivation was no longer a problem?"

Sally just stared at her friend. The tears started to stream again. "Not really. To help him deal with the smoking ban aboard the ship, I had prepared a tonic and poured a smidgeon in his morning coffee. That morning I gave him a bit more. It was a dangerous thing to do. But I couldn't deal with another outbreak by either of us."

"What would that have done? I don't understand. You're a pro with your remedies. I doubt you'd make a mistake of that magnitude. It just isn't you."

"But, Jeanne, you don't understand. That little bit extra might have made him unsteady on his feet. Caused him to lose his balance and fall."

"Didn't you say the authorities released Tyler's body so you could have him cremated and flown home? They wouldn't do that if they thought it was anything but an accidental death. So, there is nothing to berate yourself about. It was an accident!"

"Oh, Jeanne, you can always make me see reality. I've been beating myself up ever since that awful day."

Jeanne rose and returned with a pen and pad. "Here, let's begin that list," she said. "Things will sort themselves out once the details are listed in black and white." Normally, Sally was the model of efficiency. When they roomed together, Jeanne would find each day's activities pinned to the refrigerator. Social activities were listed in her day's diary, and all emergency contacts neatly listed on a 3x5 card by the phone. But this time was different. Sally needed her support in tying up Tyler's life. She needed to be reminded of the strong independent woman she'd been before Mr. Charm had swept her off her feet. The woman Jeanne knew, the one who controlled her own life.

Chapter 18

The empty bottle of Pinot Grigio sat next to her wine glass with her barely touched dinner congealing on her plate. Sally stared at the kitchen clock and sighed – it was just past midnight. The bewitching hour.

Deflated, depressed and missing Tyler more than ever, Sally looked around her dream kitchen and wished they could walk hand in hand around each room, savoring the results of a year's worth of her hard work. Work that had saved them several thousand badly needed dollars. She picked up her almost empty glass and began to walk around the two-story Tudor style home.

The purchase of the house had depleted most of Tyler's savings. Additional costs went into updating the kitchen, installing electrical, air conditioning and heating systems. With depleted savings, and additional demands on his salary, the couple struck a deal. Tyler would pay a professional to paint the outside of the house, she would paint the interior. A three-bedroom, two and a half bath house would take time. But if he could live with the mess, she would undertake the challenge. After all, she was no longer employed at Brown, Delroy and Marcus, the public relations agency where they had met. As a new bride without family responsibilities, Sally had the time to complete the project, which dragged out for a year.

As she walked to the front door, Sally turned and smiled with a sense of accomplishment that had replaced her despair as she surveyed the central hall that spread out before her. The bones of the sixty-year old Tudor house were solid, the crown molding pristine white. The downstairs hallway was bathed in a soft grey tint that opened up the narrow space.

The archway to the living room was equally inviting. It wasn't a large room but the windows gave it an airy feeling. Sally remembered one evening, before they had left for their trip, curling up in Tyler's arms on the sofa, watching the glowing embers of a fire. "Yes, we loved being here," she whispered.

As she walked up the highly polished central staircase to the second floor, she saw that here, too, the colors were glorious tints that produced the cumulative effect of a sunny springtime garden. All except the white master bedroom.

She remembered how excited they had been after they closed on the house and completed initial upgrades. With keys in hand, they walked through their very own home. Next was to move in their few possessions and give the house a fresh coat of paint. The bedroom was first on their list. She remembered rushing to the local paint store where they selected the soft vanilla white. She giggled at the memory of stripping out of her jeans and keeping Tyler focused off her body and on the job ahead. Now, as she ran her hand over the wall near the door, she recalled working side-by-side and beginning their journey of turning an empty house into a loving home.

Savoring the sight of the very first room aglow with its new coat of paint, they had rushed to the bathroom and stepped into a steamy shower. Before the paint had been washed away, Sally had climbed into Tyler's waiting arms and lost herself in a flash of passion. After one year of dating, and six months as a married couple, their love making was as spontaneous as their first time. It was one of the things she so loved about her husband. Tyler fulfilled her dreams of a loving man to start a family with.

Tears of sorrow returned. There was never enough time spent in each other's arms. It wasn't just lust. It was the way Tyler showed his love. As executive vice president of his public relations agency, Tyler left at dawn and returned home after seven each night. Then there was his travel and entertaining schedule, and lately, fewer dinners at home.

Sally knew she had married an ambitious man. After all, she had been his executive assistant at the agency for six months before they became lovers, and another year before he could get his divorce from Victoria... that woman was one piece of work! A shrew in designer clothes, she had kept Tyler shackled to his job to pay her bills.

Thinking back, Sally wondered where she was on her husband's list of priorities. Although she didn't doubt his love, Sally did question whether Tyler's financial obligations to Victoria and his two kids pushed her to the end of his list. In addition to his former family, their home was another financial obligation.

Emptying the last of her wine, Sally wondered if Tyler had resented the extra burden he assumed when they married. He never complained, just worked harder. Sally could always soothe away his tension on those nights he returned home depleted. She knew he cherished her greetings with a hug, glass of wine, home cooked dinner and his favorite cookies.

I should have helped out. Gone back to work. Maybe then I'd have had more time with the man who had been the center of my world.

Chapter 19

The wood paneled room softened the modern office of Teague, Smith and Johnson's top attorney, Jason Riley. Sally sat quietly at a small round conference table, hands tightly grasped on her lap. Breathe. Don't let her trap you into a fight.

"Welcome, Mrs. Scott," said Jason Riley as he escorted the blade-thin woman in large dark glasses to the table, guiding her to a seat across the table from Sally.

Sally watched as the woman in black took her seat, then tried to ignore her outburst. "Why am I insulted to find this... this husband stealer here? Aren't we here for the reading of Tyler's will?"

Sally sat up, stiffening her spine, and didn't remind vicious Victoria that she was the widow. Maybe the second Mrs. Scott, but most definitely Tyler's legal wife.

Jason was an old fraternity brother of Tyler's and to Sally, one of the most decent men she had ever met. Maybe not as handsome or outgoing as Tyler, but definitely a first class gentleman.

"Ladies, let's begin," Jason said as he settled between the two women and opened a thick file. "This is the last will and testament of Tyler William Scott. Briefly, he leaves his 401K investments in trusts to be shared equally between daughter, Judith Grace, and son, William John, and used for college. Any remaining funds are to be released to them on reaching age thirty. Should either of the children predecease the other, the balance of the funds will be transferred to the surviving child."

"What about me? I have to raise the brats for another ten years," screeched Victoria.

"Yes, Mrs. Scott. Tyler leaves the sum of $30,000, to continue your monthly child support payments until the children reach eighteen. Both bequests will be dispersed by me upon receipt of official invoices."

"What about the years I put up with the bastard? All those nights he was screwing around? I deserve a lump sum for pain and suffering."

"Mrs. Scott, be reasonable. Tyler settled a generous amount on you, including the house, when you got divorced."

Sally watched as Victoria reached for a bottle of water. She noticed that the widow didn't attempt to conceal the three-karat diamond engagement ring Sally knew had set Tyler back several thousand. Another gift in their contentious divorce. Would this money-grasping woman ever have enough?

"Victoria," Jason's unruffled voice firmly stopped further rantings, "may I continue? I will be happy to answer any questions when I've finished reading Tyler's will." And with that Jason wondered not for the first time why on earth his friend had married the bitch, in the first place.

"To Mrs. Tyler Scott, nee Sally Compton Scott, Mr. Scott leaves the house, car, insurance policy, and all personal property."

"What? A house and insurance policy? All I get is a measly thousand or so and care of the kids?" Victoria screeched. Turning to Sally, she continued, "I'm going to take you to court. Don't be so quick to spend your money."

"Now Victoria. Please be reasonable. We have all lost a good man. Your former husband and father of your children, Sally, her husband, and me. We have been good friends since college. I don't think you have any cause to fight this will. Not after the judge reads your divorce settlement." Jason's calm recitation of the facts stopped Victoria's tirade.

"Is that it?" Victoria snapped.

"Yes. Tyler died suddenly. However, he has always had the welfare of Judith and William in mind. Victoria, he was also well aware of your need for child support to continue to raise the children in the style they have been accustomed to."

"Yes. Yes. Yes. The children. I get it. But what about me? You don't get it. I have to live on that paltry amount. I'll pay for their college. Don't worry."

"You don't understand, Mrs. Scott. As I mentioned previously, all bills for the children's college education have to be presented to me for payment. And I will also be sending you your monthly child support payments," Jason stated in his quiet, professionally concerned tone.

Sally had all she could do not to look at the angry woman who sat fuming. Then heard Jason ask, "What happened to the generous amount Tyler settled on you when you divorced? Didn't you invest it?"

Jason's surprised tone let Sally know that had been Tyler's plan. Victoria would hopefully use the lump sum to purchase an annuity, or interest-bearing investments and in that way generate a cash stream to pay for her needs. He had told Sally that Victoria was the only person he knew totally incapable of holding down a job. Especially a marriage.

Ignoring the question, Victoria reached for her handbag. "Well then, do I have to sign something?" she asked.

"Yes, please sign next to the arrow."

After a quick glance at the papers handed to her one at a time, Victoria scrawled her signature, rose and without further word, left the office. It was as if the room warmed ten degrees with her departure.

Free of the thorn in her marriage to Tyler, Sally sat back in her chair and was finally able to take a deep breath and unclench her hands.

As he closed the files before him, Jason looked over and couldn't help noticing how lovely Sally was. He had always been jealous of his friend's second wife. She was, as the childhood saying went, sugar and spice and everything nice.

Chapter 20

The woman standing on her doorstep was close to her mother's age. Dressed in simple black pants and tweed jacket, Sally noticed that she hid an almost flat stomach, a sign of an active, not sedentary lifestyle. For someone nearing sixty, she was well preserved. When Sally dressed for the day she hadn't thought to impress anyone, and now regretted not selecting one of her better sweaters instead of the misshapen one she was wearing. Quickly smoothing the wrinkles, she held out her hand. "Ms. Fields? Do come in."

"Thank you for seeing me, Mrs. Scott. I realize with arrangements for your husband's funeral and other matters you are on a tight schedule."

"Yes. Tight schedule."

"Again, please accept my sincere sympathies at your husband's passing. My job, while necessary, isn't a task I find very pleasant."

"Right!" Sally's voice while low, was firm. "However, on the phone you sounded like you were accusing me of killing my husband."

"I get that reaction sometimes. But that isn't what we do. All I do is help to process claims."

While Sally saw sincerity in Ms. Fields' expression, she hoped this interview would be quick. As she settled her guest in the kitchen nook, Sally began to pour a pot of tea. Looking at the surprise on her guest's face, she said, "Oh, I just assumed that you would prefer tea to coffee… your accent and all."

"How absolutely refreshing to find an American who knows the British preferences."

Somewhat calmer, Sally settled more easily into the seat opposite. "So, tell me, Ms. Fields, how can I help you settle this claim?"

As she moved her teacup aside, Ms. Fields opened a folder. "Let me just reconfirm the specifics listed on the application."

"I didn't actually see the application, though Tyler did discuss it with me."

"Your husband's full name and date of birth?"

"Tyler William Scott. His forty-fifth birthday was yesterday," and lowering her head, Sally quietly brushed a threatening tear, then sat a bit taller.

"Yes. The late forties are a pivotal age for men, don't you think? I believe that's when they begin to fear growing old."

Sally watched the woman's reaction to see if she was fishing or just remarking on men in general. "I think it had more to do with Tyler's thinning hair than the year. He wasn't happy about a thin spot on the top of his head."

"They are vain creatures, and we get criticized for coloring our hair," Ms. Fields replied with a chuckle.

Sally looked at the kindly face. Maybe this visit was just a formality. *Just in case, best not let down my guard.*

"And his employment?"

"Tyler was senior vice president of Brown, Delroy and Marcus, a public relations firm." Sally took a sip of tea. Looking up she added wistfully, "He had been told that by year's end he was going to be promoted to executive VP in appreciation of all the business he brought to the agency."

"And, family? Children, siblings, any others who might lay claim to the policy?"

"Lay claim to the policy? The very same he practically bankrupted us to pay for?" Sally's voice sharpened with each word.

"Mrs. Scott, four million dollars is a large sum. The company has had long lost relatives contact us for far smaller amounts."

"We just had a reading of Tyler's will. The payment is clearly to be mine. However, to fill in all those boxes on your form, he has two children, also provided for in his will, and still under age. And a brother, who is also our accountant, and does very well on his own. He has never expected anything from Tyler, aside from a personal memento or two... which is another thing I haven't had time to arrange."

"Anyone else?"

Why did Sally feel this woman knew more than she was letting on? "How do I explain Victoria Scott, mother of two very lovely children?"

"As you see fit. This is just to make a notation should the policy be contested."

"Right!" Sally got up and began to place tea cookies on a plate sitting on the counter. Returning, she set the plate before Ms. Fields and perched on the edge of her seat. "Victoria is not a happy woman. And she could make trouble. Our attorney is fully aware of the situation."

"Not happy?"

"As you know, I'm the second wife. From Victoria's point-of-view, I'm the younger woman who stole her husband. Is that clear enough?" Just thinking of Vicious Vicky gave her a headache.

"Then I will alert the home office they might receive a call from the former Mrs. Scott." With that she slapped her folder closed. "Now that the questions are over, maybe we could just have a nice visit?"

Not expecting this from the woman she had feared meeting, Sally blurted out, "Would you like to see the house?"

As Sally took Ms. Fields through the house and proudly showed her each of the pristine rooms, she listened to a similar interest in home decorating. "You've undertaken what I know was a huge task. I complain when I have to repaint the kitchen."

"Ah, my kitchen and garden are my favorite places in my home," Sally said as she led her guest back to the kitchen.

"You garden? What a coincidence. I grow flowers. My hobby when not working," Leslie responded with a bit of pride.

"I have an herb garden. I copied it from an old Victorian book on kitchen gardens. The herbs I plant, along with other natural substances, have multiple uses aside from flavoring food."

"I'm curious. Other uses?"

"Oh yes. I flavor olive oil with thyme, rosemary and other herbs for use in cooking. Those particular herbs can be used not only for cooking but to scent lotions and creams." *Too much. Keep it simple,* she thought.

"Is cooking your only interest? Or do you use your knowledge of herbs for health or other treatments? I'm asking because you seem so knowledgeable."

"I also make topical creams to ward off bugs, and such."

"I'm semi-retired and it would be interesting to add to my knowledge of flowers," Leslie asked. "Could you show me some of your creams?"

Sally rose and walked to her pharmacopeia cabinet. On opening it she spotted a bottle of the nicotine tonic. Quickly moving it behind similar bottles, she removed two jars and returned to the table. "Here, try these. This is an aloe and rose petal cream that soothes sunburns, and the other softens roughened hands. If you give me your personal email, I'll send you some of my favorite resources."

"That would be lovely. Thank you. I may try to make this hand cream. My gardening hands could use a bit of pampering."

"Tyler also drank a mixture that I begin every day with. It contains apple cider vinegar and honey in a glass of water. It helps keep all the bacteria in my digestive system happily in order."

"I noticed that your husband had been a smoker. But in today's overly regulated world smoking is banned in most public places. Did he quit?"

"I did get him to almost quit. I believe the physical he took in order to obtain the policy will report on that." *Careful, she's fishing for something.* "Why do you ask?"

"Your policy is under the two year probation period where it can be renegotiated should the company have cause. And you are correct, his former smoking habits have already been taken into account."

The hairs on Sally's neck prickled. Fields' interest seemed genuine. All the same, she didn't have to let her know about her nicotine potion, or Tyler's renewed smoking.

"Mrs. Scott, when the policy is paid you will be coming into a lot of money. Our firm also provides financial services. Since meeting you I would be only too happy to offer you my assistance should you have questions about financial planning."

"I wasn't aware of that. If you give me your card, I will give it to my brother-in-law. He is our accountant." This turn of conversation wasn't what Sally had expected, but welcomed. It gave her the feeling that this woman wasn't out to purposely trap her or deny her claim. She was prospecting for Sally's business.

"I've enjoyed my visit," Ms. Fields said, placing her folder in her briefcase as she rose to leave. "If you would send me a copy of the official autopsy as soon as possible that should complete things."

"I was told it would take some time before the report would be released." A sudden thought sparked a twinkle in Sally's eyes.

"May I ask what you find humorous? Surely an autopsy report isn't the cause?"

"I just remembered something from the trip. Did you know that if you post a letter in the official red British mailbox on one of the landings in Antarctica, that letter will wait for a passing ship? The ship then takes it to the Falkland Islands where it is placed on a plane and flown to England. Only then will that letter be sent onward."

"Not really. It certainly isn't the most direct way to mail a letter. I wonder how long an autopsy report would take?"

"You will be happy to know that the report is issued in Ushuaia, not on the White Continent. Just as soon as it arrives I'll forward you a copy," Sally replied.

Patricia E. Gitt

Ms. Fields held out her hand. "Thank you for your gracious hospitality."

"Yes." With that, Sally ushered Ms. Leslie Fields to the front door and waved goodbye. *Okay, I've answered your questions. Now process that damn claim.*

Chapter 21

Sally returned to the kitchen a bit more settled. Her interview with Ms. Fields was simpler than expected. With that behind her, all she had to deal with was herself. She was no longer the adored wife. Nor well kissed and hugged mother. Pouring a cup of tea left cooling in the pot, she reflected on her past.

Her mother had always told her that she wasn't very bright, but with her sweet bubbling personality she would make the perfect teacher. She didn't know why her mother was determined to steer her only daughter in that direction. But Sally was determined to begin a career and prove to her mother she was more than her doll-like looks.

Throughout community college Sally had hit the books, earning high marks. Her search for employment wasn't to find a job that paid the bills, but something that engaged her mind.

An innocent, having had one boyfriend during college who had dropped her when she left, Sally was primed for romance. When Brown, Delroy and Marcus' human resource director asked if she would like to work for Mr. Scott she jumped at the chance. After all, she would be earning a fair salary and getting generous company benefits. Not to mention that Mr. Scott was a man on the rise, and gorgeous. Medium height, light brown closely cut hair and a trim body she later knew was due to an obsessive home workout routine. Once settled in she found that they worked well together. He was the concept person and she handled the execution of everything from drafting business proposals to developing and keeping track of client budgets.

Her job was hectic, and wanting to please she handled everything her boss threw at her. After six months on the job she was delighted to be promoted from assistant to executive assistant, even recognized with a small raise.

Long hours and frequent last-minute deadlines had her working closely with her boss. One evening that relationship changed, when he took her to an expensive restaurant to thank her for helping him land a particularly large account. Not accustomed to drinking half a bottle of wine, Sally remembered being a bit dizzy. When Tyler asked her to stop by his hotel room to pick up some papers, she didn't think twice. She trusted him in everything. No sooner had they entered the hotel room than he'd kissed her lightly on the mouth, and having already fallen in love with her magnetic boss, Sally allowed him access to her body and heart. It was the beginning of a secret double life she happily lived for more than a year.

Knowing that he was unhappily married gave Sally continued to hope that when his divorce became final, they would marry. She longed for a family of her own.

Two children three years apart to love, cuddle and nurture into interesting people. With the safety of a loving husband, and growing family, her dreams would be complete. Until they weren't.

Was it all a dream? Am I being punished? As Sally washed the dishes and put away the uneaten cookies from Ms. Fields' visit, a niggling thought made her catch her breath. *No, no it couldn't be. It just couldn't.*

Chapter 22

"Thank you, Ryan, for making time to see me," Sally said sitting across from her brother-in-law seated behind a paper-strewed desk. Unlike the office Tyler had at the agency, with standard office furniture and a large windowed view of the Hudson River, Ryan had furnished his office with deep green carpet and handsome mahogany furniture. It was probably because while Tyler was always out of the office, Ryan lived in his.

"Sally, you know I'm here for you. Whatever you need."

The tears threatened, and Sally nodded while reaching for the box of tissues Ryan was holding out to her. He was the patient one in the family, sensitive to other people and had always treated Sally with loving respect. He once told her that he was happy Tyler had left Victoria. That she was the one who made his brother truly happy.

"I need to talk to someone I can trust, Ryan. You are the only one who understands my financial circumstances. Tyler trusted you to not only advise him on investments, but to handle his complicated tax situation. And I'm worried about so much, especially with, ah, Victoria being the kind of woman she is…"

"Yes, Victoria, a continuing shadow over your life with my brother."

"It wasn't so bad. Tyler kept whatever conversations they had to himself. He was very sensitive to my feelings."

"Well, anyway, Sally, we do have to discuss your finances. I'm sure you know Tyler lived paycheck to paycheck. That insurance policy is a godsend, because the house is heavily mortgaged, his salary is over, and his retirement funds go to the children," Ryan said in as calm a voice as possible, knowing that this fragile looking woman was near broke.

"What about the bonus checks he gets each month for the clients he signed to the firm? Can I still receive those? At least as long as those companies are with the agency? That would be almost $5000 a month. I could live on that."

"Have you spoken to the human resources representative yet?"

The threatened tears began to trickle down her cheeks. "That isn't the only thing I haven't done. I have to go through Tyler's papers to find that damn insurance policy so hopefully, with your help, I can find out what it says. Then I have to wait for the autopsy report. The insurance agent visited and reminded me that they couldn't process the claim without it."

"Sally, you do know that even when the insurance company gets a copy of the autopsy report, payment could still be a year away. We have to get you some cash flow now."

She was grateful that Ryan had delivered this news in his usual considerate way. Reaching for another tissue, Sally waited before she continued, gathering her threatened tears, "Ryan, I haven't even unpacked Tyler's suitcase. I realize there are papers you need. I just haven't been able to even look through his desk."

"Sally, these details are crucial. Would it help if I stopped by Saturday and we went through Tyler's papers together?"

"Oh Ryan, would you? I'd be so grateful. Maybe then I can pretend we are just handling a business transaction. I used to be good at that."

Chapter 23

The breeze from the open window chilled the bedroom room and Sally automatically pulled the covers more tightly around her. Deep in sleep, she was unaware as her unsettled body began tossing and unknowingly throwing the bedcovers to the floor. Her mind in some twilight of sleep was reliving a day filled with unpleasant tasks she had begun to tackle. But having to face Tyler's death and a life with a lack of money and a future without him finally jolted her fully awake.

"Oh shit!" she exclaimed bolting upright in bed. "I killed my husband," she cried.

Leaning back into her bed pillows Sally immediately rejected the idea. Tyler fell and landed wrong. But knowing that she wasn't going to get any more sleep, Sally went into the bathroom and turned on the shower. As the hot water steamed away the fog in her mind, she tried to recapture more details of her dream. "Oh God," she prayed. "Don't let my home remedy be the cause of Tyler's death."

Sally wrapped in a robe, slammed the bedroom door open and rushed down to the kitchen. She opened the cabinet in which she kept her herbs, creams and other home remedies and spotted the small bottle hidden in the back. "There you are. The first thing I unpacked from my toiletry kit," she exclaimed.

When she thought about that morning at breakfast, just before they took off in the zodiac for the penguin nesting site, Sally remembered having doubled the dose she added to Tyler's coffee. It was her way to make sure that her husband remained in control of his nicotine cravings. *If he hadn't been on edge, he wouldn't have been so uncaring at dinner and I wouldn't have been driven to anger and that horrid fight.*

As she studied the balance of the substance in the bottle, Sally knew she hadn't administered a dangerous amount. She had marked the bottle after each dose. Since Tyler had built up a high tolerance to nicotine from years of heavy smoking, the little bit extra she gave him on the ship shouldn't have caused any negative reaction. But nicotine was a poison and if a person had an overdose, it might cause dizziness, visual impairment, even a spike in blood pressure.

"Jeanne is right. The autopsy would have shown any toxic amounts of nicotine." Somewhat reassured she hadn't done anything wrong, Sally poured the rest of the contents of the bottle down the sink and flushed it away with hot water. Then, as if the bottle were a reminder of possible culpability, she smashed it into minuscule pieces in the sink. The mess was easier to clean up than her guilt.

* * *

Well, that's it for tonight. There must be something else needing attention. Getting out of bed again and smoothing the spread back in place, Sally headed for the bathroom and before she reached the door her foot caught on Tyler's carry-on. It sat on the floor where she'd left it that first day home.

Tyler had never let her pack this particular case which he took everywhere when traveling for the agency. She remembered laughing at the suggestion that she pack it for the trip.

"So just what do you carry, love?" she said, placing the small suitcase on the bed. The first item she retrieved was his carton of cigarettes. Shaking it, she found several packs missing. Knowing his three-pack a day habit, she had packed nicotine patches for the cruise along with her nicotine laden syrup in her own toiletries case. Her research indicated that with lack of daily nicotine he could have become a complete wreck, experiencing jitters, even mood swings that would turn their vacation into a nightmare.

Laying each item of the carry-on out on the bed, she was surprised to also find a second cell phone. When turning it on, she noticed that it had an unfamiliar number. *Oh well, the office, I guess. Maybe this had an international calling card.*

The last few items were an extra t-shirt, underwear, and shaving kit... all normal overnight stuff. Just to make sure, Sally turned the case upside down and shook it. What in the world? Another surprise, a package of gum and a small tin labeled dip, fell onto the bed. Opening the small tin she gave it a quick sniff and slapped it shut.

"You dope. You idiot. Didn't I warn you not to use chewing tobacco? If cigarettes are dangerous, this stuff not only causes oral cancers, but rots the roots of your teeth."

Too angry to cry, for the first time she realized that while her husband had given her his assurances he would abide by her warnings, he'd actually ignored her. If he hadn't listened to this, what else had he ignored?

Chapter 24

"Sally," cried her mother as she rushed to enfold her daughter in a warm hug. Not waiting for Sally's greeting, she nudged her inside the front door, pulling her directly into the kitchen. "Dear, why haven't you let me visit before now? I can see how devastated you are. You may think I don't understand, but then I too became a widow in the midst of a happy marriage."

Not knowing what else to do, Sally fell against her mother, head dropping on her shoulder and gave in to her tears. "Oh Mom, I'm miserable."

"Come on, let's get you settled. How about a nice cup of tea?" As Barbara Compton moved around the kitchen and filled a kettle with water, Sally handed her a canister of tea. It was only then that Barbara turned around and finally took a good look at her only child.

"If I saw you in the market, I'd pass right by. Your lovely curly blonde hair is stringy and dark with grease. Where is that sweet face everyone has always said should have been on magazine covers?"

"Stop, Mom. I'm not the cheery daughter you've raised. What you see is me. Complete with the ripped sweatshirt, paint-covered jeans, circles under my eyes and a nose rubbed raw from tissues."

"Sally, you don't do sloppy. For heaven's sake, you even ironed your t-shirts. And gray? Never. Your wardrobe is a rainbow of pinks, greens, yellows. Happy colors."

Sally allowed her mother to lead her to the dining nook. When Barbara returned with the tea, she poured each a cup and sat waiting for Sally to say something, anything.

It had been barely a week since she had returned from Antarctica, and not wanting to hear her mother's recriminations all over again about her moving to New York, then marrying her boss, she kept delaying this visit. But here she was. What did it matter anyway? With Tyler's death there was nothing to look forward to. "Mom, I had a lot to do. And more still waiting," Sally said, dreading her mother's expected litany of "I told you so" talks.

Barbara nodded. "Honey, when I saw you at the wedding and how happy Tyler made you, I let go of my dreams for your future. That day you just radiated happiness. That's all I have ever wanted for you." Reaching out she enfolded Sally's hand with her own, and with an encouraging smile, added, "I know I was single-mindedly pushing you to become a teacher and look for that special man to build a life with. After all, that's what I did. And your father and I were happy. But that was our life. I wanted to be a homemaker. I thought that was what you wanted as well. Remember how you babysat the neighbor's kids and volunteered at the local library.

Reading your favorite childhood stories to the children? They loved you."

"But Mom, those were after school jobs. The life I wanted was in the excitement of New York City, not the sleepy suburban life you pictured."

"I wasn't aware of your plans to study accounting until you entered college. Then your father passed away and you had to go to work. I couldn't have had a better daughter. You took care of me and dropped out of college shortly before receiving your Bachelor's degree, just to make sure I was all right."

Sally was grateful that her mother wasn't criticizing her life with Tyler. Whenever she would grumble to Tyler that she wished her mother knew how happy they were, he told her that no mother wants her daughter to marry a man with another woman's children. He understood. A new understanding of this woman who raised her sparked life into Sally's empty eyes.

As she watched her daughter perk up, Barbara smiled, the first positive emotion since entering the house, Barbara smiled. "You know what? I'm going to get you out of this house. We're going to get your hair done and do some women's shopping." Barbara's enthusiasm was contagious.

"Oh yes, a mother and daughter day."

"Get yourself together and let's have some fun. And that's my prescription for the blues," Barbara said.

Sally was grateful that her mom made sure to lead the day's conversation away from her current problems. She continually peppered her conversation with commentary on fashion choices. Sally, in turn, happily shared details of her job at the agency and the joy she took being a very efficient executive assistant, a skill she continued to practice during her marriage. She also bragged that till the day they left for their trip, Tyler continued to lean on her for drafting his business proposals and acting as secretary at the golf club.

"But now that you will have to get a job, will you at least look at teaching?" was Barbara's hopeful question.

"No. I'm thinking of going on to get my degree in accounting. I have maybe two semesters left and then take the CPA exam. I'm good at supporting business people. I'm thinking I could do the bookkeeping and taxes for small business owners. Run my own little business."

"Do you have any leads?"

"Actually, one of the men at the club asked me to handle his wife's catering business. I could start there. That was just before we left on the trip. Now I think I will follow up."

"Then this dress, that suit and those easy-care polyester blouses will give you that professional look. My treat."

Laughing in delight Sally hugged her mother, feeling loved and finally accepted as an adult.

Chapter 25

Ryan sat behind Tyler's desk with Sally silently passing one folder after another across the top. "This is a copy of our last tax filing. I made a couple of notes Tyler wanted you to consider when preparing the upcoming quarterly returns."

Taking the folder, Ryan asked, "Do you have the monthly bills?"

"Here. In this folder. He paid the current ones before we left. Said he didn't want anything to take the fun out of our trip."

As he gave the statements a quick review, Ryan said, "That's good, we still have time before we have to pay these accounts. Let me take this with me. And those tax notes Tyler made. I'm going to make up a budget and see how far Tyler's savings will take you."

"I have about $15,000 in savings from before we were married. Will that help?"

"Sally, I won't let you live on the street. You can move in with me and the kids. They love you. Now, what has you in tears? I doubted you had any left."

"Children. I don't have any."

"Sally, you aren't even thirty. Let's just get you sorted. Bury Tyler and make sure you are safe. Okay?"

"Yes, sir!" Sally said with a crisp salute. Ryan would help her get her finances in order. And if selling the house and moving back with her mom was in her future it would at least be in loving surroundings. Her mom's visit assured her that she was now seeing her daughter as an adult. Finally, Sally thought, and it would give her widowed mom someone to care about.

"Sally, do you know if Tyler paid for your trip before you left? I don't see a receipt in this folder."

The tears started once again. "It was so expensive. Tyler had been saving for an entire year so he could pay for it. I would never have suggested Antarctica if I'd known how expensive it was. What with the airfare to the end of the world, then accommodations aboard the ship, not to mention all the special services, the trained expedition guides, and renting gear... it was almost two month's salary," she sobbed.

Wanting to change the subject, Ryan asked, "What's this folder, Sally? These receipts are all for restaurants and hotels. Didn't Tyler submit business receipts to the company so he could be reimbursed?"

"Sure. He took care of all that himself. Always did."

"When do you plan to visit the company? You have to see where you stand. They might owe Tyler for unreimbursed expenses, bonuses for clients he brought to the firm, even unspent funds from those he had deducted from his paycheck and placed in his health savings account."

"Okay. What else do I need to ask? Ryan, I was a lowly assistant, he had other benefits."

"Here's a pen and paper. Take notes," Ryan said kindly. "First, let them tell you what you will receive. Reimbursements not yet paid? Was he due any vacation time that they could pay you for? Would you continue to receive his bonuses for signing new clients? Did his contract include benefits for the spouse, like access to health insurance, life insurance, social security benefits as the surviving spouse?"

"I wonder what he left in his office. After we married, I only visited once. Maybe I could call his secretary?"

"Sally, that could be difficult. Why not ask the human resource representative what happened to his things? Like pictures and awards that would have been hung on the walls."

"They did send a box of things. I just haven't gone through it. Maybe tomorrow... you know, after we take care of all this stuff."

"Enough, Sally. I'm taking you to dinner. I know a really lovely quiet restaurant nearby. Let's see if we can chase any remaining tears away."

"But..."

"No buts. I have enough to begin working up a budget. You can call me if you find anything else. Okay?"

With a small smile and feeling more relaxed than she had in days, Sally placed the remaining files to the side. "Okay. And Ryan, I love you for caring."

"Sally, you must know I love you. You are not alone. We're family."

Chapter 26

It was a new day. After her first night of solid sleep since the accident, the world seemed brighter. With a cup of tea and a couple of cookies, she returned to the office and stared at a file box that had been sent over from Tyler's office a couple of days before. Did she dare open it? What would she find?

Sally prayed for a moment to calm her mind, to get a reprieve from what was going to be another emotional experience. She was grateful to Ryan for so many things. His help to figure out the financial details of her life lifted her spirits and unknowingly added a spring to her step.

"Oh, for crying out loud. I was his assistant for more than a year and there wasn't anything in his office to be afraid of." Straightening her shoulders, she lifted the lid on the cardboard box. The first items brought a smile to her lips. Lifting the leather-bound wedding photo, she slumped into the nearby desk chair. It was a dream. *Tyler, so handsome, and smiling just for me. What is that saying? That something that burns so brightly goes out just as quickly.*

The next few items were part of a desk set she had given Tyler when he signed a particularly influential new account. A soft leather folio, address book and a Cartier pen. She could hear him gush, "Honeybunch, now I will go into a client meeting with all the trappings of success." Tears began to leak as she remembered that he had enfolded her in his arms and that led to a passionate rolling around on the kitchen floor.

Catching her breath she saw the last item at the bottom of the assorted files containing his employment, retirement and financial papers, was a small black leather book. Wondering where this had come from, she opened it to find a series of colored marks next to certain notations.

Blue was next to a doctor's appointment, green next to an appointment with his barber, but what were the purple marks? While they appeared infrequently, on thumbing through other pages in the calendar she noticed they appeared about once a month. There were no appointments or meetings listed. What was it about those dates that disturbed her? Figuring that it was client related she set the little book aside. Clearing the top of the desk Sally lovingly arranged the photo and handsome desk accessories just as she knew Tyler would have. "There, all ready for you, sweetheart."

The rest of another day, she thought. Nothing but emptiness echoing in her mind as she headed for the bedroom. As if it still mattered, she took a small calendar from her bedside cabinet and marked the day. It was her diary to keep track of the few hours each month when she was likely to conceive. She had been taking birth control pills up and until she finished painting the house.

Pregnancy and paint fumes didn't seem like a good match. But since then she had been keeping track of her fertility cycle... wishing each month that it would no longer be necessary. "I guess it isn't anymore," she whispered.

I'm just worn out. I know, a stimulating shower will clear the cobwebs. No sooner had the shower wall steamed than Sally collapsed on the floor, sobbing. The rain like spray was gentle, like a soft caress. *I know he loved me. What do they say, you never regret days lost at work, but will at lost time with loved ones.*

Chapter 27

Sally dressed with care. One of her tailored suits, black of course, for her meeting with Daria Collingswood, head of human resources for Brown, Delroy and Marcus. She had prepared for this meeting, not only having typed Ryan's suggested questions, but emotionally. Now, as she clutched her shoulder bag tightly to her side as if to imprint each word on her soul, she watched the elevator doors close her in the small cubicle of space.

As the elevator to the thirtieth floor rose, so did Sally's body temperature. This visit would be the first time she wasn't an employee, but a widow seeking information about her husband's end-of-employment benefits. She knew he was a valued executive, and that thought helped restore a sense of purpose.

"Welcome back, Mrs. Scott," greeted the cheerful middle aged woman. Daria was someone Sally had a nodding acquaintance with when she worked at the agency but didn't really know. In fact, human resources was responsible for intimate details of all employees, a keeper of secrets as well. She had been wound so tightly that she forgot Daria had always seemed pleasant.

"Thank you for seeing me, Ms. Collingswood. I didn't know who else to contact."

"Daria, please. We were colleagues once upon a time."

"Yes, of course." Sally followed the woman to a small office. She was a bit easier seeing that she was welcomed, not someone to be brushed aside.

"Sally?"

"Yes, please call me Sally... not Mrs. Scott. I'm afraid hearing that will have me tear up."

"Please let me begin by offering my sympathies for your loss. It was a shock to all of us. Tyler exuded life. He will be missed."

Surprised by Daria's sincere remarks, Sally sat back in her chair and for the first time since she started out that morning felt she could handle whatever came next.

"Let me begin, Sally. The agency has Tyler's instructions to transfer on death his entire 401k investments to a trust set up in his children's names and executed by his attorney." As she removed a paper from a file folder, she turned it around. "Sally, you should read this to make sure that the attorney named is your current representative. And if the details are correct, please sign at the place marked with a sticker."

It was as Tyler had told her when as a newly married couple they set up their joint accounts at the bank, adjusted health and life insurance policies, and had their attorney write a new will, health proxy, power of attorney to name the basics of a legal life in today's complex world.

Patricia E. Gitt

"Now, your husband had some vacation time, which we will add to his final salary check."

Sally sat silently, comparing the expected amount the company was going to release to her with her monthly expenses. Even though she could squeeze a dollar so tightly it cried for help, taxes, mortgage, electric and town assessments for garbage collection all added up.

"Daria, will I continue to receive Tyler's bonus payments for the clients he signed to the firm?" Sally kept her voice soft, trying to hide her desperation. She needed more money.

"To that. Normally we do not continue to make these payments when an employee leaves the firm. However, in Tyler's case and due to the unfortunate circumstances of his death, the firm will continue to make a reduced payment for each client as long as they remain with the firm."

"Reduced?" Sally asked.

"Yes, five percent of the monthly retainer. You do understand that this is highly unusual but is being offered in recognition of your husband's dedication to the firm."

"Please thank Mr. Brown."

"Actually, it was a decision of our Board."

"Then, kindly express my appreciation to the gentlemen for their decision."

"Did you bring Tyler's company issued credit cards, office keys and identification card? I will need to have those before I can complete these arrangements."

118

"Of course." As Sally opened her bag and withdrew an envelope containing the firm's property, she also pulled out Ryan's questions. A quick glance told her that she had covered all items, except if and how she could continue on the company's health insurance plan.

"One more question, Daria. As you know, Tyler had me covered under his health insurance plan. Am I able to continue being covered by his policy?"

"Yes, but unfortunately not as an employee but as a private person. I will make the necessary arrangements for the company to contact you. They will provide options for coverage and fees. I do hope this will enable you to keep your health insurance. In this world obtaining individual coverage from major providers can be difficult."

As I well know, Sally thought. *My best course of action is not to get sick.* "Thank you. I guess that's it. May I call you if anything else comes to mind?"

"Absolutely, we consider you a part of our family."

As she gathered copies of the documents Daria had her sign, Sally shook hands, breathing a bit easier. She had just one more person to see and she could leave the building.

At the end of the hallway, Sally turned and walked past three private offices where she approached a double office space separated by a four-foot panel divider. Behind the first of the two desk spaces sat a young woman she had only met on one occasion during an office Christmas party. It was the year she and Tyler had married and this young woman was just out of college. Now, here she was a widow and that colt of a girl had transformed into a sophisticated young employee on the rise. What was the adage, you dressed for the position you aspired to? Well here was a junior executive in waiting.

Sally stood waiting for Marsha Brody to notice her and saw that the area wasn't as neat as when it was hers. She had always thought that a mark of her professionalism was the manner in which she kept not only her files, but her office space. This woman had papers scattered over her desk instead of neatly placed in folders then stacked in a tray waiting their turn. "Oh, Mrs. Scott, you startled me," Marsha said, not completely hiding the fact that she knew Sally had been waiting.

"I'm sorry. I wanted to stop by and thank you for boxing up Tyler's personal effects. Are there any additional items I may take with me?"

"I don't think so. I believe everything else belongs to the company. I'm not allowed to release address books or digital contact files. I'm sure you understand."

"Yes. Thank you again." And not wanting to stay one minute more in the presence of this obviously insincere woman, she turned and left. Not looking back, she whispered goodbye to a place in which she'd been happy. A place where she and Tyler had met.

* * *

From where Warren sat, he could see the severely dressed blonde leaving Tyler's office. While she looked like the photo Barry had sent from the ship, this woman appeared frail, thinner, somehow less magnetic than he had thought. And now he remembered her from an office party where she was introduced as Mrs. Tyler Scott.

Knowing that the bastard was screwing his secretary, who was more to Warren's taste, this woman looked like Miss Goody Two Shoes. But then again, Scott wasn't as smart as the rest of the office thought. Warren couldn't catch him at it, but he suspected that Tyler never had an original idea but farmed out assignments to his team and took credit for their work.

No sooner had the woman left than Warren got up and walked over to Marsha Brody's office. He'd had his eye on her for a while. Now it was his turn to take her to a hotel and screw her brains out.

"Is that the grieving widow?" he asked with half closed lazy eyes he knew women loved.

"Yeah. I mean yes, sir."

"Did you get a chance to offer her your sympathies? If I'd known her, I would have stopped by and offered mine. After all, your former boss was a valued executive." The rat.

"Will you be looking for a new assistant, Mr. Lazar? I think they are going to fire me and I can't lose this job."

For a woman in need of work, she wasn't so much pleading her case, as sizing him up. With that one comment, he had her number. Ambitious, unprincipled and used her sex to get what she wanted. Just perfect.

"Why don't I take you to lunch and you can tell me something about yourself. You know, your plans for the future."

"I can't leave until one. That's when I'm scheduled for my lunch hour. But lunch would give me the opportunity to fill you in on my capabilities. Mr. Scott seemed to be pleased with my work."

"Wonderful, Ms. Brody. Meet me in the lobby of the Amsterdam. We'll go to their rooftop restaurant and get better acquainted." Watching her smile reminded him of a commercial he had seen for an escort service. He was going to have to look into her background before he hired her as his new assistant at the firm. He liked to know who he was dealing with. And that was the problem with the bastard Tyler Scott. He hadn't been able to catch him at anything, except the times he left the office to screw Marsha Brody. Maybe she'd share some tidbit he could use. He'd see which way he could use her best.

Chapter 28

"Sally, I'm calling to see how far you've gotten with that list," Jeanne said. It was nine am and her day off. It was time to check in with her best friend.

"Oh, Jeanne, it is so good to hear your voice."

"Reality check first. Catching up next," Jeanne said with a smile in her voice. "I know you are counting on receiving the policy payout. But that could take an entire year. In the meantime, how about unloading that financial elephant and banking whatever is left after paying the mortgage, agent fees etc."

"Right, I have to pay a fee to a real estate agent for showing the house and readying the papers for transfer of title. I guess I haven't thought that far. Another list, this one for all the details of moving out of my first, never to be enjoyed home. Maybe the agent we bought this house with can help."

"I may have someone I can ask as well, and get back to you later this week," Jeanne offered. "But, next you have to figure out where you want to live."

"Mom said I could return home and live with her. It would save money and I could finish my degree at the local community college."

Patricia E. Gitt

"What about moving back in with me? Sharing our expenses wouldn't involve hearing your mom say I told you so. You should have been a teacher."

"She visited the other day and we finally made peace. She told me she was proud of me and that when she saw how happy I was at the wedding, realized I could handle my own life. It was a wonderful visit. But, no, I don't want to move back to New Jersey. I need to make it in New York just like we planned."

Chuckling at the thought of continuing her former youthful plans to make it in the big city, Sally relaxed. Yes, Jeanne was a comfortable roommate, also someone she loved like family. "And after we get me sorted, will your critical self go away?"

"We had fun and fit well into the apartment. I couldn't have asked for a better roommate. It will be like you'd never moved away," Jeanne said, responding to the happy thought of regaining her roommate and friend. Sally added sunshine to her daily life as healthcare coordinator spent listening to one patient after another try to pay their hospital bills.

"But it will be different. I'm a widow with baggage," Sally said. "Now all I can give you at present is a definite maybe, girlfriend."

Something in Sally's voice hinted that she wasn't as all right as she pretended. "I'll take what I can get. Just had to check in. Don't be a stranger. The train runs both ways to and from Long Island. And I do get days off."

"Promise to stay in touch. And, thanks, Jeanne. You're always there for me." Hanging up the phone, Sally realized how much she valued both Jeanne and Ryan. Yes, in spite of everything, she was loved.

Chapter 29

"Ryan? This is Jeanne, Sally's former roommate. May I stop by your office? There's something I need to find out and you may be the only person I can ask."

"It's been too long, Jeanne. Let me buy you dinner. I'll be finished up here by six and we can go to a quiet restaurant and catch up."

"I'd like that. You select the place."

"How about a little Italian restaurant a few blocks over from my office? Pipino's on second avenue and 54th street. I'll book a table in the side room. Nice and quiet. Make it 6:15."

"I'll see you then. And Ryan, thank you. Sally isn't saying much, but I think she is in trouble."

It was early for New Yorkers to be dining, and the cocktail area in the front of the restaurant was beginning to fill up. Some would stay for dinner and others leave after meeting a colleague for a drink. Still others would have a drink then rush for a train to take them back to their suburban homes.

As Jeanne entered the restaurant, the headwaiter led her to a side room where Ryan stood in greeting. "Lovely as ever. Why ever did we stop getting together?"

"Ah, your brother married my best friend and shut us out of their lives?" Laughing felt good as Jeanne's purpose for meeting Ryan wasn't a happy one.

"Caesar, a bottle of champagne." Seeing Jeanne nod in approval, Ryan then turned his attention to a woman he had wanted to get to know since Tyler started dating Sally. "You know that since my wife died three years ago I haven't made time for old friends. Seeing you reminds me of my loss. I am looking forward to renewing acquaintances."

"How could a woman not be flattered to know that a handsome, smart and above all kind man wanted to spend time with her." She had been attracted to Ryan from the first, but it didn't seem that their lives would ever cross once Sally and Tyler married. She had her life and Ryan, she knew, was in mourning for his wife.

As the waiter filled their glasses and set the open bottle in a wine cooler waiting for their refill, Ryan raised his glass. "To us. Friends."

"To friends," Jeanne echoed and with a clink of glasses some unspoken connection seemed to be moving them from barely friends to something more.

Throughout the appetizer of tomato and mozzarella followed by a pasta Putinesque, conversation brought them up to date on each of their lives. Ryan's growing financial services firm. As a CPA Jeanne knew he had started with a one-person office in lower Manhattan, and now employed sixty to help him handle the financial affairs of busy executives. Of the two brothers, Jeanne

Patricia E. Gitt

gravitated to Ryan. She always thought Tyler a bit too flamboyant and ego driven for her tastes.

"Cappuccino?" Ryan asked as the waiter cleared their dishes away.

"That would be lovely." Jeanne wanted to get to the point but hesitated. "Ryan, would you mind answering a couple of questions of a personal nature?" Seeing the puzzled expression she rushed on, "Not about you. About Tyler and Sally and their marriage."

"If I can. What's troubling you?"

"Did you know that all Sally's dreams for her marriage to the love of her life, Tyler, were wrapped up in having children?"

Ryan hadn't expected that. Should he share his confidence? It was this very topic that had haunted him ever since Tyler had confided in him a few months before he died. Concern clouded his thoughts, fearing that this wasn't going to be as easy a conversation as he had hoped.

"Ryan, are you all right?"

"Of course, Jeanne. I just did a bit of mind wandering."

"All I want to know is how to help Sally past Tyler's death and move on with her life. Oh she puts on a good show for me. But the zombie she is now isn't the woman I know."

The unbidden thoughts returned as Ryan began to replay that night and his brother's surprising confession.

128

"Don't you think you've had enough to drink?" Ryan remembered asking Tyler. They had been sitting in an eastside bar located near Ryan's office since four pm and Tyler had just ordered a third beer.

"Not nearly. I'm still coherent."

Ryan had been like a father to his younger brother. He'd instilled in him his own staunch belief in hard work, making sure that Tyler studied more and played less in high school and college. In fact, as a financial advisor with corporate clients, Ryan had spoken to the founder of Brown, Delroy and Marcus, suggesting that his recently graduated brother would be a perfect candidate for the firm's executive training program. Now, ten years later, Tyler had risen to become a senior vice president with a six-figure salary and bonuses in that very firm. But the conversation that evening still haunted Ryan.

"I've got a problem. It's taken me time and not nearly enough beer to get up the courage to ask your advice, good brother," Tyler had said.

"Now you really have me worried. I've been there for you since our parents died in that auto crash. You were ten and I was a freshman in college. By the way, since when do you need alcohol for courage?"

"It's beer, not a scotch. Anyway, here it is," he said, sitting taller on the bar stool. "You know how badly Sally wants a baby?"

"Of course. That's all she and Gloria used to talk about. You do know she is so much better than your first wife, Victoria. You finally married a really great girl."

"I guess. But I don't want any more children. Victoria's child support has driven me crazy. I needed money to shut her up. So, lately I began to take liberties at work."

Ryan had been stunned. Then, seeing the saddened expression, knew whatever Tyler was up against, he needed his help, not a lecture on business ethics.

"Nothing huge, Ryan, just a little fudging on my expense account."

"Tyler, I'm ashamed of you. If I taught you anything, it's that all you have is your good name. Fudging, as you call it, is still cheating."

"That's not my problem," Tyler said, raising his hand and signaling to get the bartender's attention. "A scotch on the rocks... only two rocks."

Ryan remembered that Tyler didn't even look at him as he continued his explanation. "This is hard enough without your career advice, big brother."

"Okay, Tyler. No more advice. How can I help you out of this fix you're in? I assume it really has to do with Sally."

"Yeah, Sally."

Tyler's look of distress hinted that whatever he had to say went beyond cheating on his expense account and Ryan had wondered what was going on. His brother was an honorable man.

"You know how nuts I was about her? How I just wanted to get rid of Victoria and marry Sally? To have her all to myself?"

"Of course. She's easy to love. Gloria and the kids adored her."

"So do I! I'd do anything in my power to make Sally happy. She saved my life of desperation." Tyler pleaded for Ryan's understanding.

"Are you planning on divorcing Sally? Is that what you wanted to speak to me about?"

"No, I don't want to divorce Sally. Don't get your Irish up. It's just that if I finally tell her no kids, she may leave me. She keeps telling me that she'll be turning thirty and her child bearing years are numbered. As an only child she dreams of having two children to spoil."

"How have you avoided the topic for five years?"

"It wasn't a problem up until she finished painting the house. She'd been on the pill. But no sooner had Sally put away the paintbrushes, she renewed her pressure to conceive and stopped all birth control. So for the past year or so I've been keeping a diary of her fertile days and found one reason or another not to have sex when she's likely to conceive."

"Tyler, that is so... I'm at a loss for words. Dishonorable, manipulative, evil! How could you do this to Sally... she's the epitome of all that's fair and sweet."

Ryan's remarks had fallen on deaf ears. "So what do you want from me? To decide for you whether or not to tell Sally? Tell her about your duplicity in preventing her pregnancy?"

Patricia E. Gitt

He couldn't remember how long the silence between the two brothers lasted. It could have been seconds, minutes or measured in quarter hours. Just like now, Ryan was stunned. "Tyler," he began as he paid the bartender for their drinks, "if it's money, maybe I can help out. If it's not wanting more children than the two lovely children you already have, then maybe you should man up and broach the subject with Sally… that is if you still love her."

"Love Sally? I'm in this desperate situation because I'm madly in love with her."

"Good. Then I'll try to help in any way I can."

As they got up to leave, Ryan remembered that Tyler asked him, "Can I call you after? If Sally throws me out you may have to let me move into your spare bedroom."

"You don't have to ask. I will always take in my baby brother," Ryan remembered answering, but now with Tyler's death, would he be the villain? Would he share Tyler's duplicity with Jeanne?

He wasn't sure how long he'd been reliving that uncomfortable evening, but looking at Jeanne, he saw her calmly sipping her coffee and waiting for his response.

That helped Ryan to make up his mind. Jeanne loved Sally, so it was probably safe to confide in her. She only wanted to help her friend. The head waiter, seeing his signal, approached. "A cognac, Jeanne?"

"Perfect ending to a delicious dinner."

When the order for their after dinner drinks had been placed, Ryan looked across the table, his attention

132

focused intently on Jeanne. "What I'm going to tell you must never be shared with Sally. Promise?" It wasn't a request.

"Of course, if that's what you wish. I only want to find some way to get Sally back to the life she had started before she married Tyler. I wouldn't do anything to hurt her... ever."

Courage, old man. Ryan took a sip of his cognac. "Tyler admitted to me shortly before their trip that he had purposely avoided getting Sally pregnant."

"What? He knew how badly she wanted children."

"Calm down. Tyler was having a hard time financially, and if they had children he didn't think he could keep his head above water."

"But Sally would have willingly gone back to work. In fact, she should have instead of parking herself in that barn. No family or friends nearby."

"Jeanne, it's all in the past. My brother was madly in love with Sally. He was afraid that he'd be embarrassed if all the scheming he did to keep up financially ever got back to his firm. I have never seen my brother at such a loss. I don't even know how he could pay for that trip."

"But he made a six-figure salary. The divorce from Victoria is settled. What else could drive him nuts?"

"Tyler wanted to give Sally a good and comfortable life. The house, country club, and this trip that she had dreamed about all her life. Jeanne, each of these are expensive, and involve more than the initial upfront costs… like mortgage, local real estate taxes, dues and the club's additional fees and assessments. That trip is probably more costly than the rest."

"Okay. Sally is just beginning to deal with her finances. Knowing this will help. I will get her to identify all her expenses and outstanding bills. Then show her that if she sells that house, she can begin anew."

"Jeanne – thank you for understanding. I think you are a treasure. Someone I would really like to know better." Ryan, seeing her smile, breathed a lot easier.

Raising his glass, Ryan toasted, "Here's to Sally."

"To Sally."

Chapter 30

Sally parked her car at the members only spot, and straightening her dress wondered why the director of the golf club had asked her to stop by.

"Sally, welcome," Steve said, rising from his table in the side room of the main club house. As he pulled out a chair for her, Sally girded herself for what she expected him to say on Tyler's passing. Not to mention how much they owed in back dues.

Settled at the table, the man sitting across from her had always treated her kindly. A bit gruff in language, he was all gentleman whenever she was present. "My dear, we are all so sad to hear about the accident. Selfishly, Tyler helped us to organize this outdated club and finally see that it was run profitably. So we are going to be missing his guidance."

"Thank you, Steve. Tyler enjoyed being welcomed into the club and wanted to help it prosper."

"Which is the reason I asked you to stop by. I wondered if you would continue to act as our recording secretary. Your notes are simple and direct which enables the Board to quickly act on the decisions made at our meetings."

"Ah...?" Sally stammered. It certainly wasn't what she was expecting.

"Of course we would pay you, say $50 an hour for your work."

Brightening, Sally thought of her conversation the day before with Jeanne. Get a life was the gist of her entire speech. "Steve, I'd be happy to help you out. And the fee is most welcome. In fact, I am thinking of beginning a small bookkeeping business. The idea came to me when Mike asked if I could look into his wife's dress business and help her organize her books."

"Bookkeeping? Tyler handled ours most efficiently."

"I know, we worked together." Sally couldn't believe the potential of Steve's offer. It gave her a sense of a future in which she would be able to earn a good living.

"So how about we come to an arrangement where we hire you on a freelance basis and see how it works out?"

Sally returned Steve's grin with a heart-stopping smile. If she had thought about it, she might not have been as effusive. Was it all right to be happy when you still haven't buried your husband?

"Steve, I would enjoy working with you again. You've always treated me with kindness. I promise to give you my best."

"Okay, how about we meet next week and when you see just what's needed you can give the board a proposal. Both continuing as recording secretary and working on our books. If you and Tyler worked together on them, I am confident we can rely on you."

"From past experience, I'd need to attend your monthly meetings and maybe work on your accounts from home. At least once I examine and set up your computer. Having worked in an office environment, I know your accounting package can be improved."

"Pretty and smart as well. Think about what we need and how you can continue what Tyler started."

As she walked to the car, Sally's mind floated free. This opportunity wasn't even a consideration. While she backed Tyler up, taking and typing up the minutes and doing the club's bookkeeping, he took all the credit. "I was just the wife. An accessory to a busy executive." As she thought of Steve's offer Sally was surprised by her eagerness to begin. "Where did timid Sally go? Well goodbye and riddance."

Chapter 31

Ryan had met a few of Tyler's colleagues at the agency for after work drinks. Now, with Jeanne's concern about Sally finding out that his brother had no intention of raising more children, he wanted to check on Tyler's other activities, fearing that he had been hiding more than avoiding parenthood.

"So, Warren, can I buy you a drink? Maybe tomorrow at the Oyster Bar in Grand Central Station. That way you won't miss your train to Westchester." Ryan had called Warren Lazar at the office but hoped to limit the time he'd have to spend with him. He thought the man a sleaze. Always looking for an angle to climb the ladder of success on the backs of others. Someone Tyler thought was out to steal his clients.

"Of course, Ryan. How are you holding up after Tyler's death? What a shock. We were all stunned to hear the news."

His hand on the phone was beginning to sweat. Prying information out of Warren may be easier than he thought. But was the odious man a source of gossip or simply the one who spread it?

"It will be good to see you again. Till tomorrow," Ryan said hanging up and now worried about what he might learn. Tyler had told him he thought Warren was a carnivore who'd eat his young if it helped him get ahead.

* * *

The Oyster Bar was a cavernous space with tile ceilings that magnified the sounds of hundreds of noisy customers ending a day with drinks or an early dinner. Ryan had made reservations for seating off to the side and gave the maître d' Warren's name.

"Ryan, old man," Warren greeted.

A bit too hearty to be sincere, Ryan thought and decided to go with the mood.

"What a nice surprise to get your call," Warren said.

"I wasn't sure if I should get in touch, now that Tyler is no longer with us. But, frankly Warren, I am curious about his last year at the firm. I had noticed a change in my brother and hoped you might be able to shed some light on his life at the agency."

Ryan waited, not wanting to rush Warren, who sat quietly. "Warren, old man, drinks on me. What will you have?"

"Oh, not necessary, but thanks." As he caught the waiter's eye, Warren said, "A Glenfiddich on the rocks."

Got you – you cheap bastard, Ryan thought. Not a bar scotch but one of the expensive brands. "I'll have the same." *You so and so. You had better be worth it.*

"To Tyler," toasted Warren. And with that out of the way, looked Ryan in the eye. "I guess you want to know about Tyler's habits at the office."

Patricia E. Gitt

"Actually, anything out of the ordinary. You have been with the agency as long as my brother and knew of his prior marriage, divorce and remarriage. In fact, I believe Sally also worked for you for a while."

At that Warren emptied his drink in one swig. Ryan promptly signaled the waiter for another.

"No. She only worked for Tyler. And your brother kept his private life out of the office. But it's no secret I wanted to bring more clients to the firm. And being a bit jealous, watched your brother closely. Mind you, for tips on why he was so successful. Nothing more." The second drink being placed before him was quickly sipped. "But you know, you see things."

"Like?" Ryan said turning his glass around to keep his fingers busy. The man was really annoying.

"Like Tyler leaving the office with his secretary, Marsha. It wasn't overt, and I'm not sure many knew. And he didn't do it often."

"Really? How often would you say?"

"Maybe every several weeks. But then Tyler relied on her for most everything. But you know, between us, Sally was far better at her job than her replacement, Marsha Brody."

With that, Ryan picked up his drink. He needed to wet his mouth, instead of giving voice to a retort that could stop this gossip from revealing more about himself than his dead brother. "Tyler often spoke of you. How you stood out at department meetings for insightful additions

140

to strategies." *I've got you, you bastard,* Ryan thought seeing the man perk up at the compliment.

"Will you be going to the memorial service? I am sure Sally would appreciate the support."

"I hope to," he said, emptying a third drink that Ryan had ordered before the last one was finished.

"By the way how is she doing? I wasn't sure it was appropriate for me to call. I can't imagine their sixth wedding anniversary trip and Tyler gets killed. Can you tell me what happened?"

"Nothing much to tell. He was taking photos and wandered off to get a closeup of a seal sunning on the edge of an ice flow. It wasn't an area he was supposed to be in and when he climbed up a snow-packed rise it opened and he fell into it, breaking his neck."

"What? Something as simple as a fall? God, Sally must have been hysterical."

"She's a gutsy gal. And she's got so many things to deal with, she just keeps moving forward." What Ryan didn't share was how devastated she still was, not sure if this bit of news would be of any help.

"Look, I hate to drink and run, but my train is about to leave. Call me, Ryan, if I can be of any help... with the memorial or anything." With that, Warren Lazar emptied the last of his drink and left.

I know Tyler loved Sally. Not wanting more children is something he should have shared before they married.

Patricia E. Gitt

But then, he agonized over telling her, afraid she wouldn't marry him. Now he was screwing his secretary? I need more proof that this isn't the product of a jealous man. Ryan knew that Tyler had never been a player. But then, sleeping around had gotten Victoria pregnant, and Tyler a life shackled to the witch.

Chapter 32

The room awaited her guests. Most of them only faces from the past. As Sally took one more look at her image in the full length mirror in a nook adjacent to the main room, she saw her mother approach with Judy and Bobby walking alongside.

"Thanks, Mom," she said while looking at two miserable children. As they approached she held out her arms and both rushed in to be held close.

"It will all be fine, kids," she said while hugging them tightly. "Today we are welcoming friends of your dad's to help us say our goodbyes. He loved you so very much and it wouldn't be right for you not to add your loving prayers as well."

Kneeling before the two children she had grown to love, Sally put on the bravest of smiles and lifting each chin looked directly into their eyes. "We are family. Your Uncle Ryan and cousins Jane and Mark are your blood relatives." Reaching for her handbag, she pulled out a notepad and wrote out her cell phone number. Handing one to each child, she saw them nod.

"Mom said you killed our dad," Bobby suddenly blurted out. "I yelled at her and she slapped my face."

"I saw her do it," Judy said, fear etching lines on her forehead, her hand crushing Sally's note. "Mom hates you. She'll never let us see you... ever."

She had to soothe their anxiety. "Why not let Uncle Ryan figure out how we can stay in touch. You now have my number and can call me whenever you want. Okay?"

"Did you kill Dad?" Bobby's tremulous voice was heartbreaking.

"You know how much I loved your dad. The trip was a vacation. Your dad was taking pictures of penguins and a seal to show you when we got back. But he wasn't looking where he was going and fell into a crack in the snow."

She saw them try to process her words and wished she could ease their pain. Tyler was the only parent to show them love. He told her that he was working on some arrangement to spend more time with them. Now that would never happen. A tear threatened, knowing that Victoria wouldn't ever let her see them again. Here she was a widow without their child, and now she would be losing these two wonderful children as well.

Sally turned to see her mother approach. "Mom, would you take Bobby and Judy over to sit with Jane and Mark?"

As Barbara took each child by the hand, she turned and whispered, "Honey, if you need rescuing, just look my way and I'll distract the person hogging your attention."

"Thanks, Mom." It took a moment and she again turned to the children. "Go over and join your cousins. After this is over we can all go out for ice cream." As she saw some spark return to their faces, she calmed. Somehow she would stay in touch, just as Tyler would have wanted her to.

One last glance at the mirror and Sally entered the back of the gathering, where her mother walked to her side. "Mom, I'm waiting for Leslie from the insurance agency. I called her last evening and said that I had just received the autopsy report from the Argentinian Consulate here in New York and I'd be here most of the afternoon if she wanted to come by for a copy."

"Why in heaven's name would you invite her to a memorial service for Tyler? Isn't she investigating his death so as not to let her company pay the policy?"

"Actually, I don't think she's that heartless. As she explained it, the government wouldn't have let me cremate Tyler and bring him home if there was any doubt about his death being an accident. It's just completing the paperwork so they can release payment."

The room began filling up and as Sally shook hands with each arriving guest she tried to remember where they fit in Tyler's life. Most she had met when she was Tyler's assistant. However, there were a couple of new faces. "Oh, Ryan, do you know that gentleman over there? The one who looks like he stepped out of an ad for the latest hot Porsche?" she asked, pointing out the slim, navy suited man with crisp white shirt and designer tie.

"I think Tyler and I once had drinks with him. If memory serves his name is Salvatore, something or other. He was a slick one. Perfect in appearance but you wonder if you were talking to a well-rehearsed actor. I doubted he has a sincere bone in his body. Let me investigate."

"Ah, Mrs. Scott," Leslie whispered as she entered the room. "I'm glad to see you feeling a bit better. I was pleased to get your invitation and pay my respects."

"Thank you, Ms. Fields. I left an envelope for you with the gentleman at the front desk. I must admit I scanned it but the details of the coroner's report eluded me."

"Actually, I will be submitting it to our office. These forms elude me as well."

"Why not get yourself a glass of wine. I'll be making a short speech in about ten minutes."

"Sally," Ryan said and taking her elbow turned her away from the room. "I'm going to mingle a bit more. That man is John Salvatore and he works for Warren Lazar. Don't worry, sometimes another man will say things he wouldn't dream of saying to a woman. Okay?"

Something's got Ryan's dander up. Giving him a reassuring smile, Sally turned back to greet the next guest. "How nice of you to attend, Ms. Brody. I am sure this is a difficult condolence call. Please get a glass of wine. And thank you for coming all this way to pay your respects." As she watched the woman, four years her junior, with a long legged body sway away toward the bar, she couldn't help wondering what it was about the young woman that bothered her. There was something about her expression – while properly stoic it looked like she was hiding something. *Not now. Don't go looking for trouble.*

It was time. Picking up a glass of white wine she had only sipped, Sally walked to the front of the rows of chairs and stood facing the room. The guests who hadn't already settled in their seats, did so quietly. The gathering was small. Outside of family, there were fewer than a dozen people from Tyler's firm.

"Friends and colleagues of Tyler's. Thank you for helping me honor my husband and when I'm done I'd like to invite anyone who wishes to come up and add a word or two of their own.

"As most know, I met my husband while working at the agency. I was privileged to have worked with a professional team, members of Tyler's group. By way of background, Tyler's favorite sport was golf, his love of his job was all consuming, and his desire for a happy personal life made living with him a joy. His brother Ryan will now say a few words."

Leslie had been mingling and listening to the men talk among themselves in low voices, hearing one single out a tall young woman, saying she had been more than a secretary, often seeing her leaving the office late with her boss. The inference was confirmed when the other man said that he would see them every so often entering a mid-range hotel several blocks from the office. Since the hotel was not known for either its cocktail lounge or restaurant, the assumption was an assignation. He wouldn't have thought that, but he'd witnessed them entering the establishment almost monthly.

"Ladies and gentlemen," Ryan began. "My brother was ambitious to a fault. But a kind and fair-minded man in every way. We are gathered here to say goodbye, hear the comforting prayers of Father Patrick, and see that the family can lay Tyler to a loving rest. So please raise your glasses and share my toast – Tyler, may you rest in peace."

Later, the memorial service now over, Sally sat with a freshened glass of wine, her mother off somewhere discussing the actual burial with the funeral home director, the children sitting off to the side waiting for them to leave.

Ryan sat next to her, and placing an arm around her shoulders gave her a little squeeze. "It went well. And that Salvatore was everything you pegged him as. And gossip. Nothing to worry about from that quarter." Standing, he walked to the bar for a glass of wine.

"Mr. Scott, I'm going to be leaving," Leslie said while shaking Ryan's hand. "I know you are helping Mrs. Scott work her way through her grief and responsibilities of winding up her husband's affairs. Please tell her that I promise to call when my agency has reviewed these papers. I'm sure everything is in order. Not to worry. As we Scots would say, folks die, but the toon clock still chimes. Or, life goes on."

"Thank you for coming. I know Sally appreciates your kindness during this difficult situation. Please do call me. I understand that your firm also does some financial planning. We may be able to work together when things get settled." *It never hurts to be nice before that check is written*, he thought.

Chapter 33

"Jeanne. Lovely as usual. Thanks for meeting me. Why is it we never spent any real time together? You know, for fun," Ryan asked, hoping that Jeanne would look favorably on him after he shared information he gleaned from Warren, and from what he'd picked up during Tyler's memorial service.

"Ah." Jeanne sighed as she picked up her cup of coffee. They were seated at a neighborhood coffee shop during an early afternoon break from both their hectic days. Ryan from finalizing a financial report for a client and Jeanne taking a break from counseling a patient about her outstanding hospital bills.

"Sorry for calling you away from your office, but I had to ask you a favor. I'm afraid I'm caught in a bit of a dilemma."

"Ryan, I watched you yesterday at the memorial service as you circulated, chatting up one guest after another. I am assuming that the tall brunette you were talking to was Tyler's extracurricular interest?"

"How did you know he wasn't faithful to Sally?" Ryan asked, surprise written over his normally smooth face.

"I didn't know. You just confirmed a suspicion I had. It was something Sally said."

"Yes, Marsha Brody, Tyler's assistant." As he searched Jeanne for her reaction, he added, "Does Sally know?"

"From what Sally has shared about her intimate life with Tyler, he couldn't look at her without jumping her bones. So if what you shared before about his not wanting more children, I wondered if he was simply, how do you men state it? Meeting his needs with someone else? Is this what you want to tell me?"

"Not entirely. At the memorial service, did you happen to notice a tall thin man who looked more like a fashion model than an executive?"

"Yes. Good looking... poured into his designer suit wearing a tie heavier than he was? Why?"

"His name is John Salvatore and he told me he's being given a couple of Tyler's clients. He will be reporting to Warren Lazar."

"Well, it didn't take the firm long to fill Tyler's shoes," Jeanne snapped.

"I don't know if Tyler mentioned Lazar, but he was up for the same promotion and Tyler never trusted him. But Salvatore was a font of gossip. He hinted that Tyler was successful in gaining new clients because he had been bribing them."

"Fits the stereotype for his profession?" Jeanne snapped. "PR is about lies and coverups."

"It can be. But the good firms maintain a higher set of standards, although sometimes it's the clients who are the underhanded players, " Ryan said.

"So this Salvatore... did he know you are Tyler's brother?"

"Yes, and he was filled with false remorse over his death, all the while telling me the gossip he'd heard around the office. It was like he had to prove he was the better man."

"And this Marsha was top of his list of tall tales?" Jeanne asked.

"Yes, more importantly, he said it was suspicious that Tyler, of all his colleagues, was the one who consistently signed major clients. Jeanne, he all but accused Tyler of other underhanded tactics."

"Tyler was aggressive, but underhanded? Sorry, Ryan, but I didn't think your brother was all that bright to pull anything underhanded and get away with it."

"I believe he was insinuating that Tyler had some quid pro quo arrangement to get them to sign."

"You've got to be kidding. Did this guy tell you what kind of scheme Tyler was pulling?"

"Yes, free membership in a golf club or local city men's club."

Jeanne couldn't help but giggle. "You know Sally did those books. And she is as principled as a nun."

"My dilemma. Should I investigate him? Find something to shut him up? Or should I share my suspicions with Sally before I go any further?"

"Ryan, you can't tell Sally anything like that until she's gotten past settling Tyler's affairs. She's barely holding herself together. Don't you do their taxes? Can you check his business deductions? Maybe get duplicate receipts from the firm telling them that you need it for estate filings?"

"I can try. I have to protect Sally from my brother's less than credible behavior."

"Maybe I can have Sally stay with me a night or two. Knowing about her feckless husband, I might get her to open her eyes. As far as Sally is concerned, the man she married was a saint. Smart, ambitious and besotted with her."

Jeanne's sarcasm wasn't lost on Ryan. "You apparently didn't think much of my brother," he said, voicing his surprise.

"It's not that. I guess I have always wanted Sally to see the man in all his dimensions. They had such a passionate relationship. I'm just afraid of her reaction when she has her eyes opened and finally sees the man she married."

"Jeanne. That's a bit harsh. Tyler loved Sally. Though I must confess, even before they met he had developed into somewhat of a chameleon."

"In what way?" Jeanne asked.

"As a kid, he never seemed to fit in. As he got older I noticed that he always stood apart as if to study those around him. In fact, strangers would take that silence for intelligence and leadership capabilities. Maybe that's why he moved up the career ladder so quickly," Ryan said, somewhat surprised by this unexpected thought as to his younger brother's character.

"So how do we approach Sally? I can get her to talk. But you are going to have to find some proof before we bring any of this to her attention."

"Right. Back to receipts. I'll start there."

* * *

"Sally," Ryan said, speaking as calmly as he could over his office phone. "Can you remember who Tyler saw at the office before you left on your trip?"

"I think so. Why? I doubt It's important now."

"See if you can remember and call me back. Not to worry, I'm just trying up a few loose ends. Hugs."

Not two minutes later his phone rang and Sally's number popped up. "That was quick. Did you remember something?"

"Yes and no. Marsha Brody, that leggy brunette we met at the memorial service, was his assistant. She would most likely have been the last person to see Tyler. Is that what you were looking for?"

Ryan sat mute. "Yes, Sally, that will do."

"A bit cool for my taste," Sally added.

"One more bit to add to the file, Sally. Not to worry. Just putting the pieces of the office together." With that Ryan hung up and stared out the window, trying not to think about the disappointment in his brother.

Chapter 34

"Jeanne, I've brought a variety of clothes not knowing what you've planned. Your promise of a couple of days acting like tourists in the big city was just the diversion I need. If I haven't told you before, I love you."

"I've got it all planned. There is a new costume exhibit at the Metropolitan Museum, a Bloomingdale's cosmetic promotion where we can be transformed from dreary to dreamy women of the world. And I've tickets for the ballet at the cinema," Jeanne said pointing to a coffee table piled with brochures.

"Why are we seeing the ballet at a movie theater?"

"I forgot you've been out of the city for ages. Instead of paying high prices for seats in the stratosphere, you have a front row seat in comfortable lounge chair seating and are close enough to see the faces of the performers. And our tickets are for the Bolshoi's Romeo and Juliet. You'll love it."

"You know what I'd really love to do, and it's my treat."

"What?" Jeanne asked as she poured glasses of Sally's favorite wine.

"Dinner at that old New York steakhouse downtown. The one you and I celebrated my engagement at."

"Great idea. Let's go there tonight. The first day of our holiday. Here's to enjoying ourselves like we used to," Jeanne said as she hoisted her glass in a toast.

"Cheers," Sally responded. "Oh, I feel years younger already."

Sally was sure Jeanne was up to something. When they were roommates, she limited her social schedule to an occasional dinner at a good restaurant and maybe one Broadway show or ballet every couple of months. Both were on restricted budgets but for Jeanne to have already sprung for the cost of a ballet... even if on film, was out of character.

* * *

"Hey Jeanne," Sally called into the bedroom. They were getting ready to go downtown for the steak dinner. "Instead of going out tonight, why not sip our drinks and have a girls' night of gossip and catching up."

Jeanne emerged from the bedroom, surprise written on her face. "Are you sure? I thought you'd want to be out and about. Something to take your mind off your troubles."

"I thought I'd want that as well. But the truth of it is I have to puzzle out the rest of my life. Would you mind helping me put the pieces together? Wine and nibbles would, of course, help", Sally replied with a hopeful smile. "Or maybe a fattening pizza?"

"Great. Back to the bedroom and into a comfy caftan," Jeanne replied.

The wine bottle sat on the coffee table, filled glasses raised. "To us. To solve life's problems. To put the pieces back together," Jeanne said.

"Okay, before we order that pizza, what aren't you telling me? I know you, and when you organize a social weekend, you are avoiding quiet time alone," Sally said, as she watched Jeanne take a larger than normal sip of her wine. "Out with it."

"Even if it's something you won't believe?"

"Uh oh. What have you gotten into? Do you need me to bail you out of another credit card overcharge?"

"I should be insulted. Long ago, I gave up carrying over balances on my credit cards. Now I keep track of my charges and stop when I don't have enough to write a check and pay my statement in full. That's thanks to you, Sally. If I can't write a check, I don't make that purchase. Not even for a bagel," Jeanne snapped.

"So what's so sensitive that you have to bribe me with wine?"

"Oh, Sally. I hope I'm wrong.

"Remember that fashion plate, John Salvatore from the memorial service? Well, he hinted to Ryan that Tyler was so successful in gaining new clients he had to be bribing them with golf club privileges." Jeanne sat back and waited for her dearest friend to explode.

Instead, Sally started to smile. "Isn't he the one who took over some of Tyler's clients?"

Nodding in agreement, Jeanne was further surprised to hear Sally laugh. "Jeanne, I do the club's books. Tyler never even broached the subject of using the club for entertaining a client, prospective or existing. Is that all?"

"Unfortunately not." With that pronouncement, Jeanne refilled her empty glass while noticing that Sally had barely touched hers.

"Don't you dare hold back. It seems as though you and my brother-in-law have been conspiring behind my back."

"As with Tyler's bribing clients, I have no proof of what I'm about to divulge. Did you know that in spite of your trying to have children, Tyler didn't want any more?"

"Come on, Jeanne. He wanted what I wanted, a family. That's the main reason we bought that house in Great Neck. It has a great school system, room for a family and has parks and facilities for kids."

"As I said, I've no proof. Ryan and I were just trying to squelch gossip." Jeanne's comment ended the discussion. She was satisfied, watching a calm Sally reach for her drink.

"Okay. Now that you've cleared your conscience, girlfriend... Pizza?" Sally said, her humor restored. Jeanne and Ryan were just being faithful friends.

"And what has you grinning now? All those calories you are about to devour?" Jeanne asked.

"Ah, it's interesting that you two have been meeting. I know you both want to protect me." As Jeanne left the room to call for their dinner, Sally thought, *Jeanne and Ryan, Now that would be something to cheer me up.*

Chapter 35

Up early to put her clothes into the washer, Sally's thoughts returned to her conversation with Jeanne. Once she'd convinced her that the unfounded rumors about Tyler using the golf club to sign new clients were just that, they had spent a wonderful couple of days together enjoying New York City, from a downtown steak dinner to visiting uptown shops. Jeanne had even convinced her to purchase a new dress that wasn't black.

With an empty laundry basket in hand, Sally walked by the entrance to their home den and noticed the box of Tyler's things sent by the firm. She had already gone through it, but something made her walk over and dig down to the bottom, where in addition to the small diary she pulled out Tyler's business card case. Carrying both to the kitchen, she set them on the table and walked to the stove, putting the kettle on for a cup of tea.

Settled with a couple of cookies and her tea, Sally picked up the card case and remembered when she stopped into that small leather shop on Madison Avenue and purchased it as a first anniversary wedding gift. Money was tight and at $70 that was more than she should have spent. After all, she no longer had her job, and the only cash was what Tyler gave her for household expenses.

The worn leather showed heavy use, but on closer inspection she noticed an irregular outline of something other than a card raising a welt on the smooth leather surface.

What the… was her instant reaction as she pulled out a foil packaged condom. *We haven't used birth control since I finished painting the house. Why would Tyler keep this in his card case?* A sudden thought and her hand began to tremble. No. Not possible. Not Tyler. He was as avid a lover now as he'd been when they'd been dating. Why would he need to have sex with anyone else? On closer inspection she noticed that the package was crumpled, not crisp like new. "That's it. Maybe he just forgot to throw it out," she said letting her heart return to normal.

Not ready to go down that road of suspicion, she opened the monthly diary to the beginning page. January was marked with cryptic notations and colored pencil marks. The most frequent color used was green. Thinking back, she remembered Tyler having taken a trip to California to see a client. He said he was looking forward to the two days during which he wouldn't be wearing his heavy winter coat. Well, it could have been on those days.

The color blue was the next most frequently used and it appeared on the second and fourth Tuesday of the month. Of course, Tyler's appointments with his barber. He'd been fastidious about his hair. He'd told her that just because it was thinning was no excuse to get sloppy.

Feeling more relaxed, she next saw a couple of dates marked in purple. No notation to tell her the significance.

As she turned to the month of February, the blue colors appeared twice, the barber appointments, and only one of the dates marked in purple. Curious.

Sally placed the diary off to the side. Something was tweaking the corners of her mind. As she nibbled at a shortbread cookie, Sally let her mind roam free.

The diary was new. Even when she had worked as Tyler's assistant, she had never seen this little book. A thought came, so abhorrent she spilled her tea as she rushed from the table and back into the den. Booting up the home computer, Sally used Tyler's password to access his office files. "Shit! And double shit!" she exclaimed. The password no longer worked. The office had closed out Tyler's workstation. "What else have they prevented me from accessing?"

Chapter 36

Her five year old Subaru sat across the street from a two story colonial house that fit neatly into an upper middle class neighborhood. It was a stark comparison to Sally Scott's modest home on a working class street. This wasn't part of her job for the insurance company, but Leslie liked Sally Scott and was curious about the former wife. After yesterday's memorial service, she was leaning toward the conclusion that Tyler Scott's death was accidental. The autopsy report Sally had handed her was being reviewed at the home office. But Leslie was almost certain that it contained nothing to provide grounds for denying payment on the four million dollar policy.

The invitation to visit from Tyler Scott's first wife was a surprise. When Edwin had told her that the first Mrs. Scott called a second time to inquire the date she'd receive her portion of the policy, Leslie's antenna went on alert. The policy was clearly written with one beneficiary, Mrs. Sally Scott, legal wife of the deceased.

As she gathered her tote bag with tape recorder nestled inside, Leslie left her car and walked up to the front door of the house. At the first knock the door was opened by a caricature of a woman: skinny, shoulder length straight black hair and dressed in black slacks and silk shirt. She was facing a real-life Morticia of *The Addams Family* cartoons.

"Mrs. Scott, I'm Leslie Fields of the National American Insurance Company. We spoke briefly yesterday."

"Yes. Come in," was the woman's abrupt reply.

Leslie was accustomed to being treated like a guest when visiting someone seeking money from her company. What a surprise to be directed to a wooden chair in a living room of upholstered furniture. On closer inspection, the sofa, chairs and settee didn't look as if they had been used. Certainly curious, she thought, when there were two children under the age of thirteen in the house.

"Ms. Fields. Let me make myself perfectly clear. I am the wronged party. That woman stole Tyler from me and the children. She doesn't deserve even one penny of his life insurance policy."

"I can understand your concerns. Maybe you can tell me a little more about your marriage. Something to help support your claim?"

"Oh, just ask your questions. I've nothing to hide."

"Would you mind if I recorded our conversation? Your answers will be forwarded to the claims department. It's a more accurate way to convey your information." Leslie was studying the woman for any signs that she was reluctant.

"Go ahead!"

"I understand that you and Tyler were married for five years. That your divorce was finalized six years ago. Is that correct?"

"Yes."

"Would you describe your husband as a good provider? Someone who was ethical, responsible and a good family man?"

"Ms. Fields, he cheated on me. He's scum. Does that answer your question?"

"How about his professional life. Are you still in contact with any of his co-workers?"

"One or two… socially. What does that have to do with my claim?"

"Would you please give me their names? I am trying to better understand Mr. Scott's professional life and speaking with people he worked with will be a great help." *I certainly won't be contacting anyone he worked with, you greedy piece of work.*

"I'll send it to you. Give me your card… you do have a business card?" was the woman's arch reply.

Leslie reached into her tote and pulled out her card case. Now, after meeting wife number one she had nothing but sympathy for the dead man. Who could live with Victoria Scott and not want a divorce? "I look forward to hearing from you. One last question. When was the last time you saw Mr. Scott?"

"The day before he left for that god awful trip. Tyler hated cold weather. But that bitch made him travel all the way to the ends of the world for a trip that cost the price of a year's college education. She doesn't deserve to live, let alone get paid for killing my husband."

Leslie hurriedly gathered her things and reluctantly held out her hand to say goodbye. The bony hand with sharp nails gave hers a quick shake, and coolly rushed her to the door.

As Leslie stood outside the house, she wondered why it had taken Mr. Scott only five years to leave. Comparing the value of this well-finished home in an upper middle class neighborhood with that of Sally Scott's barely furnished one, Leslie now knew that Tyler Scott practically bankrupted himself to get rid of the first wife. *I probably would have too.*

Chapter 37

"Thank you for seeing me on short notice," Jeanne said as Ryan gave her a hug and led her to a chair opposite his large desk. A desk cluttered with files. "What a nice surprise. May I get you anything? Water, coffee or tea?"

Jeanne's arrival snapped him out of his serious mood. He enjoyed this woman and was pleased she felt comfortable enough to stop by on short notice. "Jeanne, you can always see me. You are never a bother."

Drawn by his welcome, Jeanne wondered if she was falling in love. It had always been easy between them. *Stop it. Today's visit isn't about me.* "I realize this is a last minute thing… but the truth of it is I would like to get a better picture of Victoria. I can't ask Sally and until the claim is resolved the grasping witch will continue to lurk in the background."

It took Ryan by surprise. Jeanne wasn't family, yet she knew unpleasant details about Victoria's impact on Sally. Settled behind his desk, he took a moment before answering. "There is really no way to describe Victoria. You've seen her at her best," Ryan said with a sad smile.

"Okay, maybe tell me a bit more about Tyler and how a man I liked could have married, let alone lived with that woman? Sally used to call me after she picked up the kids and I could never understand how those two lovely kids turned out the way they did living with that woman."

"Let me tell you about my younger brother. He charmed everyone he met. But when he met Sally, that breath of fresh air, he was happy probably for the first time in his entire life."

"His chosen profession would suggest that he was outgoing, friendly and gathered friends easily. That was the man I knew."

"Ah, you've met Sally's husband, not the boy," Ryan commented with a smile that reached his eyes. "Sally wouldn't have recognized my brother as a child. He couldn't seem to fit in at school. He was too short for basketball, too thin for football and not coordinated enough for tennis or track. So you might say he was a bit of a loner."

"That certainly isn't the image I've gathered from listening to the men at the memorial service. They seemed jealous of his ability to sign clients, his way of charming everyone, and the ease he seemed to have in handling his business responsibilities."

"I'm not sure what I'm going to share with you is relevant. So, if I say something is not to be shared with Sally, will you honor my request?" The charmer had been replaced by the canny accountant.

"You know Sally is my best friend. I would never divulge anything to upset her. By the way, that rumor from

Salvatore. The one in which he accused Tyler of bribing clients with golf club membership? When I shared that with Sally she laughed, saying not only would Tyler never do that but she kept the books."

"Did you mention his other tidbit about Marsha and Tyler?"

"I said he hinted at an affair. She seemed to just pass it off as gossip."

Ryan Scott relaxed into his leather chair, and after a moment he decided that Jeanne knew enough and would probably benefit with a little of his family history.

"Tyler was his own best creation. Upon entering high school he embarked on a series of self-improvement classes. First, to develop a scrawny body into a well-muscled young man. Not an oversized muscleman, you understand. But he did transform enough so that his shoulder bones could no longer be seen sticking through his shirts. I'd watch him pose in front of his bedroom mirror in a t-shirt, admiring his toned torso. Next, he took up public speaking and while painful to my reticent brother, by his senior year in high school he was able to join the debating team. Tyler then studied acting and eventually became the successful businessman he had envisioned as a teen. And last, but probably most important, that was the man Sally met and fell in love with. The man you knew."

"Are you telling me that your brother was a fake? That Sally bought his act hook line and sinker? A person can't simply make themselves into an entirely new entity.

There are personality quirks, native abilities, and those wouldn't change even if the person appeared to be outwardly different."

"No, my brother was only too real, he just polished what he felt was an inferior mind and body. And he wore that appearance like those fashionable suits. However, his success was due to knowing his limitations, and a drive to succeed backed by hard work. That was the man Sally met when she became his assistant. But that man wasn't warm, didn't trust anyone outside of me. You see, our parents died in an automobile accident when I was eighteen and Tyler only ten. I doubt if after their deaths he ever experienced feelings of being loved."

Ryan sat pondering his next words. "I was in night school and holding down a full-time job to keep the roof over our heads. Now that I think back, we lived separate lives.'

A look on Ryan's face had Jeanne's attention and she heard something probably not meant for her. "That may explain why he married a woman like Victoria." It was a naked thought.

"And Sally?"

"She was a gift. When he fell for her, Tyler began to trust that he, along with his secrets, was safe. You see, she loved him unconditionally."

"Look, someone doesn't have the career he had and not have been smart." The more she heard, the more puzzled she became.

"Tyler did. For years I watched him maneuver his way up the corporate ladder. He'd never admit to me his fear of being found out. Nothing but a fraud."

"After working in a hospital dealing with patients and their financial problems, I am pretty good at figuring people out and I don't get it."

"Tyler directed others, that was a skill. He found ways not to do the actual work. I can't believe no one caught on. He would assign others to prepare for client meetings. Sally told me she wrote most of his proposals. Once, I heard a colleague grumble that they asked Tyler to contact a top business reporter so he could tell a prospective client they had been in conversation about the client's firm. But Tyler refused. I personally doubt Tyler would have done anything like that. Growing up, I tried to instill in him a certain honor, reminding him that all he had was his good name."

"Sorry. From what I overheard I think some knew exactly what your brother was up to. But apparently his position with the company kept him safe from complaints."

"Maybe you're right. But it won't matter now," Ryan said. "Is there anything else?"

"One more little thing. I'm afraid it's that matter of his relationship with that secretary. I know you mentioned it. But I still don't get it. How could he be blindly in love with Sally and cheat on her?"

It took Ryan a long minute to reply. "As I mentioned previously, Tyler didn't want any more children so on those days during Sally's monthly cycle, he'd bed Marsha."

"Was this a fling?" Jeanne's wrinkled brow spoke volumes of disapproval.

"Not even a fling from what my brother shared with me."

Shaking her head, Jeanne wondered how any husband ever explained that to himself and still believed he was faithful to his wife.

As she rose to leave, Jeanne held out her hand. "Ryan, thank you for your honesty. I don't know if anything you shared will help Sally, but it does help me."

"I admire your loyalty to Sally. To me, that is a sign of a trusting and loving soul. Selfishly, I hope you will include me in your close circle of friends."

As he stood and took Jeanne's hand to lead her to the office door, she turned and gave him a wide happy smile. "You already are."

Chapter 38

"Thank you," Sally said to the pizza delivery boy as she handed him a twenty dollar bill, a tip worthy of a far larger order.

Plopping the hot box on the kitchen counter, Sally poured her second glass of wine. The bottle sat witness to her plans of indulgence in alcohol and fat, trying to soothe her raw soul.

Certainly not on any diet I've read, she thought as she took her first bite of the sausage laden pie. Hot, a mouth burning sensation that had her gulping her wine. "Sally, girl. Time to fess up. Tyler wasn't perfect." But nearly so, she sighed. Taking another smaller bite of pizza, she put the rest on a waiting plate and picked up her glass. "To me. The future. And burying the past."

If only I could, and the tears began to flood her eyes. Several hours later, not even the empty bottle of wine sitting abandoned on the counter had dulled her pain. The pizza, an unappealing mass still in its box, was long forgotten. A sudden queasy feeling had her rush to the hall bathroom and promptly throw up. Weak, with head in her hands over the toilet bowl, Sally let her tears run free.

I must be wrong. Pulling herself to her feet Sally dragged herself upstairs to their bedroom. She was determined to prove Tyler's fidelity and began hunting through every pocket, drawer and cabinet, searching for proof of her faith in him.

Tyler was a neatnik. So it didn't take long to reach into each of his suit jacket pockets. Pants had to be taken off hangers and searched as they lay on the bed. A crumpled pair of slacks waiting to be taken to the dry cleaner had been pushed to the back of the closet. Picking them up, Sally froze as she saw another of those foil packets falling to the floor.

She couldn't get her mind around it, knowing it wasn't meant for their use. When and why would Tyler cheat on her? Another idea pushed its way into her thoughts. As she rushed to the other side of the bed, Sally pulled open her bedside table drawer and grabbed a little diary. It was her personal calendar. The one she faithfully marked, tracking her monthly period. Those few critical days in her cycle circled in pink. Dates she would be likely to conceive. All her hopes and prayers had been focused on having their child.

As she carried the calendar back to the kitchen, she prayed that his little black book wouldn't show purple notations on days that coincided with her fertile ones. Stumbling into the room, she grabbed the book sitting next to the card case.

"Okay. Prove I'm wrong. I'm a widow, mad with grief and simply jumping to conclusions." But when she opened up

Patricia E. Gitt

to January and compared dates, it was only too clear. Tyler hadn't just strayed from the marriage bed – he had avoided her on those precious few hours when she'd be likely to conceive. That lie pushed everything else from her mind. They'd talked for hours about their child. Readying the house and their lives to welcome a baby that would make them a family. "No, I had talked nonstop. Tyler listened."

Dropping onto the floor, Sally was comatose. The expected tears didn't flow. Feelings of hate didn't emerge. She sat empty. Cold. No thoughts of what she was going to do.

* * *

"Ow," Sally said as she tried to sit up after a night in bed, not remembering having gotten there. *I don't know which end to take to the bathroom first.* Carefully, holding her aching forehead, she hung her legs over the side of the bed and after waiting for the pulsing pain in her head to subside, headed for the bathroom. First, wake up, she decided and positioned herself under the shower head, turning the cold water on full. Shocked awake, she stood shivering, which was somehow preferable to the hangover.

Dried and wrapped in a heavy terry cloth robe, Sally gingerly made her way to the kitchen and the coffee maker. *If I could infuse caffeine into my veins, I would.* With eyes closed, the tormenting thoughts of the night before began to trickle back. *A piece of foil packaged rubber doesn't mean Tyler didn't love me. For Christ's sake, we screwed like bunny rabbits.* The buzzing coffee pot knifed into her brain and without adding her customary cream and sugar, Sally sipped the hot brew.

No, but the systematic way he avoided making me pregnant… that was a betrayal of the deepest kind. If he wasn't already dead, I'd kill him. And the tears started all over again. Her nose running along with her eyes forced Sally to reach for a tissue and realize she didn't really know the man she'd married. She had loved him blindly.

The coffee pot was down to the last cup as Sally emptied it and sat back down at the kitchen counter. Who would know about Tyler's devious actions? His infidelity, if it existed. *His making me believe he wanted children and avoiding me on any day that would make my wish come true. Not only devious, it's evil. Why couldn't he tell me his concerns? We discussed everything. Yeah, all except our children.*

Tyler didn't have any close friends. If I didn't know about his deception then I couldn't have mentioned my fears to Jeanne. She is almost witch-like in her ability to get me to talk about anything bothering me and would nag me until I shared it with her.

The headache was gone, but her nose was raw after a night of blowing it. Her eyes red from constant rubbing to make the tears stop.

As if a door had opened in her mind, Sally saw her life with Tyler. It was just the two of them. Ryan and his wife Gloria, before she had died, and their two children completed their circle. Sally had practically given up spending time with Jeanne and spent the entire six years focused on her life with her husband. She had married the man of her dreams. Realization of what she didn't know left her chilled.

I can't move forward without knowing, she decided as she put her coffee mug in the sink and left to pull herself together. She had an important phone call to make.

Chapter 39

"Sally, this is so nice of you. I haven't had one of your scrumptious home cooked meals in ages," Ryan said as he sat back in his chair wearing a warm, satisfied grin.

"I was lonely," Sally said, enjoying this quiet man's company. "You know, Ryan, the truth is you have always treated me as one of your family. I just wish we had seen more of you and the children since Gloria passed away."

Ryan reached over the table and gave her hand a squeeze. "You are my family. Probably my favorite member since my wife's tragic death." Ryan sat for a moment lost in thought. "I still can't wrap my head around her death. How someone so vital, who took care of herself with regular exercise and control of her diet… not only hers but mine… could have a massive stroke and pass away before the ambulance even reached the hospital."

"Tyler told me she had a weakness in her carotid artery and that bleed is always fatal. Gloria's passing was as sudden as Tyler's. To make it harder, there is a niggling part of me that still thinks it's my fault." Seeing the horror on Ryan's face she knew she had to share her secret guilt.

"I'm going to tell you something that may change your opinion of me. It's about Tyler's addiction to smoking." *Well, in for a penny in for a pound.* "Knowing that there would be a smoking ban while on board ship, I researched nicotine and its addictive powers. I read about a tonic that could be prepared and if used sparingly... and I mean sparingly, it would provide enough nicotine to combat Tyler's withdrawal from cigarettes. You see, during this past year, he had returned to his three-pack a day habit."

"A tonic? Isn't nicotine a poison?"

"Yes. But my research included actual measurements of proper dosages. So every morning at breakfast on our trip, I'd pour a minuscule amount of this preparation into his coffee. My fear is that since he continued to wear those patches, the ones to help give up smoking, I may have given him a bit too much the morning of his fall."

"Too much? You just told me you carefully measured each dosage. So why this guilt?"

"Please understand, Ryan. I loved Tyler with all my heart and soul. But the evening before we had a really bad blow-up. As I was going to sleep I attributed his unusual temper to his not smoking. So that fateful morning I increased the dosage. Side effects include dizziness. My fear is he fell into the crevasse because he lost his balance."

"Sally, stop it. The autopsy report cleared you. Even without it, the coroner and medical examiner had to have seen the nicotine patch on Tyler's arm when they examined the body. And, I am assuming they would have followed up with a toxicology screening. Since the government released Tyler for cremation and allowed you to bring him home, your little nicotine tonic couldn't have been a factor."

Taking in a deep breath, she looked up and saw the conviction on her brother-in-law's face. If he and Jeanne believed her innocent of any wrongdoing, why couldn't she?

"Sally, knowing how much you loved my brother made me so very happy. Did I ever share that with you? How could your love do anything to harm him?"

She felt his reassuring presence. He was her family, and she realized loneliness was a new sensation for her. She had gone from her childhood home to Jeanne's when she began working at the agency, and moved in with Tyler, who had made her feel loved and safe.

"Ryan, we didn't really have any social life. Tyler's friends were limited to the country club and the office. I guess more acquaintances than true friends since he never invited any of them to the house." Now the other shoe to kick this nice man with.

"Here, let me fill your glass. By the way, I prefer white wine. How did you remember?" Ryan asked.

"Ah, because that is my favorite as well and Tyler always asked me to have a bottle chilled when you came over."

The silence that followed made her uncomfortable. Ryan was too well mannered to bring up anything but pleasant memories of the past. His reaction to her confession about her tonic had surprised her. With a healthy sip, she placed her wine glass by her plate, took a breath. It was time.

"Ryan, can we be honest with one another?" Her question was more a plea.

"Of course, Sally. I love you. In addition to loving my brother, I'm not sure you realize how much Tyler loved you. Or that your love for him helped to chase away ghosts from his past."

"You mean Victoria." With that ugly name voiced, Sally reached for her wine to cleanse her mouth.

A shocked expression caught her by surprise. "Ryan, she was the evil source of all Tyler's problems. She left him without a penny. Drove him crazy with constant haggling over the final divorce and kept him from his lovely children."

"Sally, sweet girl. You don't understand. Victoria was merely a symptom."

As she sat there and listened to Ryan explain his brother's rough early life, including bullying in school, lackluster grades in college, and total lack of self-worth, for the first time Sally's eyes opened to the flawed man she'd married.

"So you're telling me the man I married was a man of no talent or abilities? Ryan, that isn't true. How could he have built a successful career, earned a six figure income, with frequent bonuses I might add, if he wasn't smart and well grounded." Momentarily forgotten were her fears prompted by that horrid foil packaged surprise. She had to defend not only the man, but their marriage.

"Calm down. Yes, Tyler accomplished a lot. You, my dear, helped him begin to transform from posing as the successful executive into becoming one."

"But... but..." she stammered.

"Listen carefully. Tyler was a success, but without you he'd never have believed he deserved to be."

"This is a lot to take in. But Ryan, he also lied to me." There, it was out. Would he tell her the truth behind her suspicions?

"Lie? Tyler?"

Ryan rose from the table and taking her hand led her to the living room. "Okay, Sally, out with it. You have something on your mind. You can tell me anything. Anything at all... even if it's about my brother."

Where did she begin? With the condoms? With her diary duplicated in the one she found among his office things? "Ryan, was Tyler unfaithful?" Whew.

"Yes, physically but not emotionally. Sally, the act of sex for men is a physical need. The overused metaphor is 'an itch to be scratched.' Tyler was so very much in love with you that yes, he had infrequent sex but didn't believe he was being unfaithful."

Rage, confusion, betrayal all fought one another before she could even frame a reply. "We had the hots for each other, why would he need to find relief with another woman?" An odd and aberrant thought ghosted into her thoughts. "Or, was it a woman?"

Ryan's laughter wasn't what she had expected. Here she was learning that her husband couldn't keep his zipper zipped when he traveled or was away from her. What was she to believe? It was just sex?

"Stop it. Stop it. How could he? Who was his go to when not with me?"

"What has you asking me these questions? Why don't you believe me when I tell you that your husband thought the sun and moon rose and set with you?"

Sally got up and went to the office. She was going to show him the diary. The one with her monthly cycle clearly marked, and Tyler's with coordinated days. On returning to the living room, she dropped one of the packaged condoms and both diaries into Ryan's lap. "Here. Can you explain these?"

It didn't take long for Ryan to look at the diaries and when she saw the regret written on his face, knew her suspicions were verified. "So? Tyler is dead, it shouldn't matter… but, Ryan, it does. Was I a fool? Did I even know the man I married? Apparently not from what you have already told me." Dejected, Sally slumped down into the cushions of the chair, bracing for whatever Ryan would tell her.

"I wasn't going to ever tell you this. Tyler should have explained his thoughts about having children before you bought this house. Just after you found it, we had met for drinks and he said all you talked about was having a family. But, after Victoria robbed him of almost all of his money, he didn't know how he would support them."

"Wait just a minute. I could have gone back to work. We didn't have to go into debt with a mortgage this size. If he'd only talked to me we could have worked something out," Sally cried.

"Who did the family accounts, Sally? You or Tyler?"

"I set up the household accounts on our computer. Tyler took care of everything else. He said it was complicated having to keep business and personal expenses separated."

"And all his credit cards? Who paid those invoices?"

"They were all business related." Seeing the serious look on Ryan's face she now wondered if she knew the entirety of their financial picture, or only the part Tyler wanted her to see. "I'm a grown up, Ryan. You do our taxes, tell me what I apparently don't know."

"Let's start with your anniversary trip to Antarctica. Were you aware of the costs? Or how Tyler paid for it? Sally, that was over $40,000."

"Tyler told me that he had points to use and that would save us almost $1000 in airfare."

"Sally, he charged the entire trip to a new credit card, one he apparently didn't share with you… and he only paid the minimum each month."

"That's crazy. The interest alone would amount to more than the trip. He wouldn't do that."

"Sally, you are aware that Tyler's 401K is to be distributed to Judith Grace and William John on his death."

"Of course. He loved his children."

"And that the life insurance policy he purchased was his disciplined way to plan for your future? By paying the policy premiums regularly he was setting money aside for your life after his retirement. He was afraid if he wasn't forced to save on a regular basis his spending habits would prevent you from having a comfortable retirement."

"That we never got to enjoy."

"Sally, the premiums on a four million dollar policy cost thousands all by itself. Then there is the mortgage, costs to prepare the house, real estate taxes, upkeep, local water and electric bills. Not to mention the country club. Sally, these all add up. How do you think even with Tyler's salary he could keep this up?"

"That's why he was always working. He needed those bonus checks for each new client he brought into the firm. His salary wasn't nearly enough."

The tears began to flow, as she mentally tried to tally the costs. Instinctively she knew she had avoided asking how Tyler could afford the house. It was as if a shut door had slammed open.

Ryan left her alone with her tears and on his return handed her a glass of chilled wine. "Here. Sally, it's time to move on. Let me help you, please."

"And his itch? Who did he scratch it with? Marsha? That'd be convenient," Sally snapped.

"Yes. You met her. She used him to get ahead in the firm. It didn't mean anything to either of them."

"Equality in the office at last," Sally replied and as she sipped the wine, her mind cleared. "Ryan, I need to think about all this. I believe that you and apparently my husband believed his behavior was meant to protect me. For all my I can do anything attitude, this is going to challenge my belief in myself."

Ryan rose, and leaning over to give her a kiss on the cheek said, "Sally, please don't go through this alone."

Nodding, Sally watched him leave and with his departure, so did her dreams of that perfect life she had with Tyler.

Chapter 40

It was nearly midnight and after poring over her household expenses, completed with Ryan's new information about Tyler's secret credit card balance, Sally decided she had to not only sell the house to pay off all outstanding debt, but needed to find a life beyond loving wife to the myth of a man she had married.

Once again her nerves were causing nausea and rushing to the bathroom, she promised to see the doctor for medication. If she was broke, she didn't need to be sick as well.

The following morning found her body cramped, having fallen asleep with head on arms atop a pile of financial charts. "Caffeine. Or I won't be able to make any sense of this stuff," she muttered, pushing the paper aside. She barely remembered printing all the information, preferring paper for reading the spreadsheets than on the computer. Paper allowed her to slow down her brain long enough to mark critical data. And with that Sally headed off to the kitchen and the coffee pot.

"Okay, Sally Compton Scott. Money. Where will it come from? Right. Work. What rock did I hide under not to remember that I'd have to earn my way through life?

Come to think, I was Tyler's secretary at the golf club and did their books. I just never got the credit... or paid. Steve has my proposal, so maybe I do have a way to keep my body and soul together."

As she sipped her first cup of coffee for the day she grabbed a pencil and her shopping list, scratched out 'to buy' and wrote in 'to do.'

"Settle with the insurance company. Pay off all bills. Set up automatic deposit in a new account for the balance of Brown, Delroy and Marcus payments on Tyler's end of employment contract. "Shit. Then what?"

I need help. A sensible mind to organize my life. Picking up the phone she called the one person honest enough to give her unvarnished advice. "Jeanne, can we meet? I need your common sense to help me make some serious decisions." The phone was glued to her ear as she listened to Jeanne's reply.

With a luncheon set for the following day, Sally washed her hair and pulled out her best suit and heels, ready for her life-defining conversation with the person who knew her best.

* * *

"I'm glad you suggested we meet at the apartment," Sally said as she hugged her best friend. "If I didn't know today was your day off I would have suggested another time."

"In your honor I ordered up. Sushi from your favorite take out place," Jeanne said.

The remnants of lunch left on the table, Sally decided to share Ryan's unexpected information. "You remember Ryan? You two were trying to protect me from the truth?"

"Of course."

"What?"

"We have been kind of seeing one another."

As she saw her best friend's dreamy expression, all thoughts of herself were forgotten. Wanting to know more, she gushed, "Oh Jeanne, he's perfect for you. Kind, exudes love, and misses his wife dreadfully. You'd make him so happy. You'd get him back into having a life outside of work. I swear that man hides in his office."

Jeanne just kept smiling.

"Cat got your tongue? How did you get together? When and where? Are you serious or just visiting the idea? Jeanne, I need to know. This is the happiest I've been since Tyler died!"

"Sally, when you got back from Antarctica you were a mess. We were both worried about you. I called Ryan because in addition to being worried about your frazzled state, I hoped he had some information to help me get you to take charge of your life. So he invited me to dinner." The smile on Jeanne's face said it all.

"So how long has this been going on? How many times have you been together? Spill it." Sally reached for Jeanne's hand, giving it a friendly squeeze. "I love you and Ryan, and hope this is a new beginning for your both."

"Enough about me. What has you rushing back into the city? Don't get me wrong, I love seeing you."

Sally didn't take long to tell Jeanne about Tyler's duplicity with regard to having children, or that he took his monthly relief by screwing his secretary.

"Sally, he wasn't perfect. You were the only one who thought he was," Jeanne replied.

"Well, that's history. My problem is, where do I go from here? At present I'm almost broke. Have no job, well maybe the prospect of earning some money. What do I do?" This time, her question was not that from a grieving widow. It was from a person who was determined to build a new life.

"Okay. You've tackled your financial picture, so now to straighten out your life. Sally, don't hate me, but when you fell for Tyler you forgot all about you. Your dreams of getting your CPA credentials. I'm not sure you thought beyond that. Whether you'd work for an accounting firm or in the accounting department of some company. You were so close to accomplishing your goals and just let them go."

"There wasn't time for me to think about finishing my education. First I had to be there for my mother. Then, my life was intertwined with Tyler's. Jeanne, you can't imagine all the things I did that didn't have the label housewife."

"Like what? Painting a house?"

"No. Of course not. Now I understand why Tyler was so intent on signing new clients. We needed money. All those little assists to his career. Framing new client pitches, reviewing his monthly reports, acting as secretary at the club, and anything else that enabled him to focus on prospecting and signing clients for the firm."

"I'm amazed at how long it took you to even realize that you were still his executive assistant, with benefits," Jeanne said, totally amazed by her friend's blindness to the man she married.

Ignoring the sarcasm, Sally wanted to get back to the now of her life. Where was she going and how was she going to get there. "Look, I have some of the finances in order, and there's more to deal with than adding two plus two. I've a mortgage, normal bills, and taxes are coming up. But Ryan has been helping me get that information together. So, I'm thinking that finishing my education should be on top of that list."

"Not only school. Where are you going to live? You can bunk back with me. I'd love having you to come home to. You sometimes finished up early and I remember the apartment welcoming me with all kinds of delicious smells from the kitchen. That's something take-out doesn't provide."

Laughing together felt like old times. "A few more credits, then I can get that CPA. Thinking back, did you know I used to help my mom's friends balance their checkbooks. Some are widows and thought of me as their friendly accountant."

Turning to Jeanne, Sally's mind no longer focused on food, debt and Tyler. It was the most relaxed she had been since boarding the ship for Antarctica.

Chapter 41

"So Leslie, we met one last time. At least in this case. The autopsy report and the firm's decision on the Scott policy."

"I've taken an inch tape." Seeing Edwin's grin, she amended, "Tape measure to this case. Okay?"

"Glad your investigation hasn't hampered your Gallic tongue."

Leslie loved nattering with Edwin, and purposely sprinkled her language with colorful, older Scottish phrases. After all, they were more interesting than plain English.

"I'm all ears. And personally, after meeting and talking with varying people in the deceased's life during his last weeks of life, I've concluded his death was an accident."

"It seems the autopsy report agrees. Here, read it for yourself."

"Why not give me the agency's final decision. It's less scientific and gets to the point. Will they or won't they cut that four-million dollar check?"

"The body showed a broken neck. The scalp and skull showed no signs of trauma. The only odd thing was that he wore a nicotine patch, but it didn't add anything to a negative toxicology result. To continue, the man was in otherwise good health, strong bones, well-manicured fingernails, external genitalia and anus were normal."

"That's certainly a colorful report."

"The body's position and photographs taken above and below the place of the fall, showed no questionable footprints or other signs in the fresh packed snow, clearly indicating the man had been by himself at the time of his fall. And due to the obviously indicated cause of death the examination only included a toxicology screening of blood, urine, bile, liver, brain and gastric contents, confirming no additional or unusual contributions."

"So we pay up?"

"Yes. Leslie, would you like to call the widow? I'm sure she would appreciate a woman's sympathetic voice when telling her she will get a check in sixty days and asking where to have it sent."

"Aye, the wee widow. Tis folly tae live por and' die rich. Translation, I will offer my wishes that she use the money wisely and enjoy living. That is what you mean, isn't it?"

* * *

The phone had been ringing and Leslie was just about to hang up.

"Yes?"

Unlike the now familiar voice answering, this was firm and somewhat rushed, nothing like the distraught widow

Leslie had gotten to know. "Mrs. Scott, this is Leslie Fields."

"Oh yes, Ms. Fields. What can I do for you and the National America Insurance Company?"

Smiling, Leslie was only too happy to reply. "It's what we can do for you, Mrs. Scott. The autopsy report has been reviewed along with my report and the company will release payment to you in about sixty days."

Silence greeted her. "Mrs. Scott, are you still there?"

"Yes, yes Ms. Fields. I'm so very relieved."

"I'm glad at least this news is positive. All I need is the place to deposit the funds. Have you a bank account or brokerage account where we can direct payment?"

"You aren't going to believe this. I don't know. May I call you tomorrow? I have to check with my accountant."

"I fully understand. This is a large sum and should be treated carefully. You have my number."

After agreeing to call Mrs. Fields in the morning, Sally slumped down on the bed. She had been packing up Tyler's clothes in preparation for donating them to the local church. He'd been a clothes horse and his wardrobe, while not extensive, was in excellent condition. It was a first step in clearing out the house.

"Whew. I'm not going to debtor's prison or have to live with Mom." Now what?

* * *

"Hi, Ryan. Success. I just hung up on Leslie Fields of the National American Insurance Company telling me they need a place to send my four-million dollars. I can't believe it. After all this worry, self-doubt and stress, I can afford a life. More importantly, I have time to figure out what my life will be. My new life. All mine."

"This is the best of news after the stress of the past weeks. Let me get back to you. First we need to set up a new account in your name at the brokerage firm to receive the funds. Then, we have to meet and discuss how to invest them in the short term so you not only keep them safe but have money going forward."

"Ryan, I've told her I'd get back to her tomorrow. Will that be possible?"

"All right. I'll set up an account with the firm I use and email you the information. You will need to register with them, but you can start by calling my representative and he will walk you through it."

"You are the best. In the meantime, back to packing up Tyler's things."

* * *

With her tea sitting on her bedside table, Leslie Ann Fields released a satisfied sigh. The month-long investigation into the death of Tyler Scott and the validity of his widow's claim on the four million dollar life insurance policy was finally settled.

Underlining a diary notation, "love blinds" she thought that this case was one for the books. With information overheard at the funeral, she had discovered that the widow had seen her husband through rose colored glasses and then spotted her diary note written later that day, "the glasses cracked".

Picking up her pen she wrote, "Good for you. You are reclaiming your life." She had seen weaker women collapse and be forever soured on men and life. But she recognized the fighter in Sally and knew she'd be all right.

At first she was skeptical of Mrs. Scott's innocence. While she looked like a young, blonde, not too bright second wife, Leslie quickly learned that her tears were real, and subsequent questions had discerned a sharp mind.

As with every case, Leslie updated her list of things learned in the past and present for future assignments. It read:

Not every claim is fraudulent

Not every beneficiary is clueless to the amount of the policy payout

Claimants have complex relationships with the policy holder

Age doesn't determine intent or level of intelligence

Tears can be real and provide insight into relationship between beneficiary and policy holder

Don't forget to see behind the face presented to the public

Trust my gut.

Chapter 42

"So Ryan, no taxes on the four million. What a delight to keep the government's grubby hands off my tragedy."

"Sally, I'm also suggesting you place two million in tax free municipal bonds. Whatever they pay, you will get interest twice a year and the money will be working for you."

"Can't I keep a healthy chunk in, say, a money market account? You know, for cash flow? Or how about an annuity with a monthly payout?"

"Sensible plan. And it will keep you from blowing it."

She couldn't help laughing. "Remember me? Sally, a housewife who could squeeze a nickel?"

"Yet another gift you brought to my brother, thinking of money as security. That without it you had less freedom to make personal choices."

"I never gave a thought to the balance, Ryan. Good idea. And I will already have a small retainer from the country club to cover minor personal expenses. It's something to start out with. Then I can spread out paying the costs of an apartment renovation and furnishings. So there should be enough of a cash flow to cover the apartment, and monthly minor expenses of electric, cable etc."

As she hung up the phone, Sally was for the first time confident she wasn't going to end up in either debtor's prison or staying at her mother's. Next, Deidra.

"Hi, Deidra. This is Mrs. Scott. I was wondering if I could stop by. I am thinking of selling our house. You know it better than anyone else. Also, I appreciate the referral. Caroline was terrific."

* * *

"Mrs. Scott, you and your husband certainly brought this house back to its former glory as a solid, warm and well-designed home. In fact, from my point-of-view, your minimal furnishings are also a blessing should you want me to show your house."

"I certainly spent the past year painting, some wallpapering and sewing curtains. As for the kitchen appliances, Tyler gave me a free hand in selecting the best available. Not in price, mind you, but in basic reliable performance. In fact, I have a binder with all the paperwork for each appliance which should help the new owner in operating and servicing them.

"Now that you have toured the house, do you think we can get more than the $750,000 we paid for it?" Sally hoped she wasn't sounding too needy, but she would do whatever she could to maximize the sale.

"A couple of suggestions, if I may. First, would you be able to clean up the front yard and maybe add one or two low bushes by the front entrance? That will set off the charming Tudor design. Another would be to place new towels in the bathrooms. Just to make them look a bit crisper."

"Those suggestions don't seem too onerous. Anything else?"

"No, and I think you have added another $100,000 to the value of your home. If I remember correctly, this house had been an estate sale and somewhat rundown, which was the major reason for the lower price in this excellent neighborhood. What with outstanding schools, community services and upscale residents, you did very well."

"When do we start? I'll need a week or so to empty closets and find a new home."

"As long as you place all boxes and things in the basement, I can start showing next week."

"Thank you, Deidra. Will you keep me posted as to when anyone wants to come to the house? I'll make sure I'm someplace else."

"Happy to. And, Mrs. Scott, the house looks lovely. I'm just sorry for the reason you have to move."

Chapter 43

"Hi, Mom, how would you like to meet me in the city? I've some shopping to do," Sally said and was pleased to hear her mother rush to agree. "How's tomorrow morning? I'll meet you at Penn Station and we'll have coffee."

* * *

They were seated in a nearby Starbucks and Sally waited until her mother had taken her first sip of coffee before telling her they would be looking at apartments.

"You what, dear? You are apartment hunting here in Manhattan? Why? You could come home and live rent free while you get straightened out."

Sally really did love her mom and hoped she would accept her desire to start an entire new and independent life. Something she had tried to do when she first moved into New York City. Then she had roomed with Jeanne. Once again she would be looking for an apartment. It was another first step. "I have an appointment to meet a real estate agent at a new building. It seems that they might be agreeable to negotiating on price simply to begin filling the building with tenants."

"And how did you find this person? Are you sure she's reliable?"

"Yes, Mom. I called the real estate agent Tyler and I bought our house through. She told me that her firm has offices in the City and offered to set me up with someone she personally vouched for. She said the agent was also a recent widow and didn't have children. So you see, she starts out ahead of some man without a noodle of an idea of my needs."

In front of a building still undergoing final stages of construction, stood a slim woman about five-foot tall with close cropped dark brown hair, dressed in business attire and carrying what looked like a tablet, large handbag sitting securely on one shoulder. If Sally remembered correctly, she had a similar shoulder bag when she began working for Tyler. It was her tool kit with everything from wallet and makeup to an extra pair of shoes. How she hated running for a bus in heels and would change out of her sneakers once she arrived at the office.

"I understand today is an introduction to prices and what they will afford you in a two bedroom apartment, Mrs. Scott. Am I right?" asked Caroline Ayers. "Were there any other specifics we might consider?"

"For starters, I like this area of New York. I will be attending college to complete my degree and Baruch is nearby. I don't want to be in the high rent district, preferring a low key life. What I'm looking for is a space to make a home, complete with a kitchen to cook in...

Yes, I cook," Sally added seeing surprise on Caroline's face. "I will be entertaining and working from home, so a dining area and space to set up an office complete with computer etc. is on the list."

After a moment's thought, Sally added, "A balcony would be nice but price may preclude that extra."

"Good. Being specific will save us a lot of time. Let's talk about prices first. A range of what you expect to pay will help me select options to fit your budget."

Sally hadn't realized just how expensive it was going to be to live in Manhattan. Even with the sale of her house, she wouldn't be able to afford more than a studio. Feeling her mother nudge her elbow, she saw a glint in her eye. Leaning down to hear better, Sally hears her mother whisper, "Don't forget you are going to get four million dollars. That should help enormously."

Laughing, she looked at Caroline. "Let's not worry about price until I see what my money will buy."

* * *

They were back in the house Sally grew up in, shoes kicked off and sharing a pot of tea after a hectic day. "I'm glad you decided to come back with me," Barbara Compton said, "I've kept some of your things in the bedroom. At least you can go home tomorrow with clean underwear."

"Mom, what did you think about today's adventure? Out with it. You haven't asked me even one question about what I've got in mind. Unusual for you, I must say."

Sally's tone, while soft, didn't hide her curiosity. Her mother was nothing if not opinionated.

"An interesting trip watching you take charge of your future. At two-million dollars give or take a million or so, you surprised me at how efficiently you've handled the challenge. I'm interested in knowing if you preferred the first new building complete with roof deck, pool and gym, or that brownstone with a garden in the back? I know you liked your herb garden."

"That's all? No reminder that teaching in New Jersey would be a quieter and easier life? That you aren't a grandmother with children to spoil?"

"Gave that up when you married Tyler. And you aren't even thirty. Time for a new man in your life and children. Not to worry. I'm keeping my options for you open."

It was good to laugh with her mother. There were a couple of times in years past when Barbara's preconceived idea about who she was gave her agita. Now where did that Italian cliché come from? Maybe the fog was clearing at last.

"What is that saying, Mom? Busy is as busy does? Well in the past few days, I've certainly been busy."

"So which apartment do you like best? The high rise two bedroom, or the duplex in the brownstone with room for a home office and a lovely backyard?"

"First, I'll have to check with Ryan that keeping the price close to two million will give me leeway to completely build and furnish to my heart's desire. My problem is, how much of that four million policy check will I be able to keep? Ryan told me that I won't have to pay any taxes. However, there will be real estate agent fees to sell the house and purchase the new one. Do I take out a mortgage to be able to invest the rest? And I still haven't earned one penny. So what will my monthly costs be?"

"I'm not surprised about the thoroughness of your checklist. I assume Jeanne helped you think things out. So which one?"

"I'm tired of the work required by a house. I love the idea of twenty-four-hour security, modern telecommunication connections, and a handyman to repair whatever breaks. As for the charm of the brownstone and possible garden, I'm not sure I will have time. What with school, the two clients I already have, and maybe your friends will continue to need me for their financial bookkeeping."

"What a smart girl I raised. Of course they will want your attention. One is currently working with the son of a friend, and she complains about his niggling questions about her travel to spas."

"Ah men, they are so clueless," Sally quipped and both broke out in laughter.

"So the big city accountant will live in a sky high building and be safe from the outside world," Barbara said. Squeezing her daughter's hand, she added, "Honey, please don't isolate yourself in that tower. You're young and need to add fun to that life you are building. Promise me you will."

"Mom, I want to try and stay in touch with Bobby and Judy. What do you think? I know Victoria will block that, but I am hoping Ryan will get legal permission to arrange for the kids to visit him. And, who knows, they have my phone number, maybe they will begin to reach out. I do love them." Feeling her mother kiss her forehead, Sally knew it would all work out.

"I'll help in any way I can. It would be criminal to leave those two lovely children alone in that woman's hands. They need to know they are loved," Barbara said. "And, I will have grandchildren," she added with a broad smile.

It was another challenge to her newfound life. Yes, a social life. Maybe she'd expand her world when she began to work with local business owners. Who knows where their connections would take her. With Jeanne all but occupied with her relationship with Ryan, she knew it was time to strike out and find new social circles to join. A book club? Graduate school might be in the offing if she wanted a more complex group of clients. Travel? Oh yes, travel.

"And once settled, I'm going to have you, Jeanne and Ryan as guests to a home cooked dinner. My closest family and best friend," she announced, wondering why she never hosted them all together before. No longer loving blindly, Sally was going to treasure the family she had. And parties – small gatherings where she would mix new friends and expand her social circle.

"Mom, I'm going to be okay," she said, and giving her mother a huge hug, believed every word.

Chapter 44

Midnight came far too quickly. For a three bedroom house in which she had really lived in one bedroom, office, and kitchen, she had accumulated boxes and boxes of stuff. It would be the mover's problem to cart the furniture along with over fifty boxes of assorted sizes into their truck and then unload them at the new address.

Sally had planned it out on graph paper. If all boxes were placed in the middle of the long living room at the new apartment, she could unpack slowly as she went about reorganizing her new life. The decorator had already installed her minor changes and painted. The building agreed to install her desired floors, kitchen appliances, laundry and bathroom selections, in lieu of lowering the price of the co-op. Sally would decorate after all her belongings were put away. She had never had free rein to design a home from scratch and wasn't exactly sure what style of furnishings she'd settle on. Her own meager possessions held emotional value but weren't enough to say she had a personal style.

The remaining two slices of pizza stared at her. But the hunger gnawing her stomach could no longer be denied, so she reheated the cheese and sausage slices left from dinner before in her toaster oven, her wedding gift from

Jeanne that she used each morning to heat muffins or to reheat something for lunch. It was the last thing to be packed away.

* * *

She hadn't expected to get any sleep, and turning to look at her bedside clock saw that it was five am. *And so it begins.* Her mom would be at the apartment by nine, awaiting the arrival of the movers. If anyone could organize the placement of boxes and furniture it was Barbara. She'd driven Sally's dad crazy when he decided they had to move to a larger house. As Sally remembered their frequent "discussions", Barbara usually got her way and since it would be left to her to unpack, Sally's dad gave in.

There was no need for a temporary place to stay, as the building already accommodated early tenants and had quickly made the upgrades she ordered. Sally didn't mind the unfinished hallways in the building, as long as she was snug in her own apartment.

After a slow steamy shower, Sally dressed in a clean pair of jeans and new t-shirt. She wasn't going to move into her ritzy Manhattan apartment looking like an escapee from a natural disaster. She had already washed the paint-covered clothes and planned to use them as cleaning rags.

Taking the empty pizza box out to the garbage bin waiting by the curb, Sally looked around the sleeping street of similar Tudor style homes. They had been built in the early fifties and by now each had acquired the personality of its owners. One featured a front yard fit for a botanical gardens ad, another had a pristine closely cut lawn and deliberately planted and trimmed bushes. Her own house looked like a family lived there. Greenery almost haphazard but pleasing to the eye, and the stucco that still had the fresh look of a recently painted exterior. *Oh my. That's all I thought about. I should have been getting a job.*

"I forgive you, my love. I should have known you were reluctant to start another family. But you were my everything," she whispered. She had been deliriously happy. Now she knew that Tyler's straying wasn't all his fault. She had unknowingly contributed to his angst. "I have to take blame for pushing you into a crazy work cycle to keep us from bankruptcy. And into that woman's arms. You will always be in my heart. Rest in peace."

The sun was just over the roof of the house and cast a glow over the setting. Sally smiled. *I could have happily raised our kids here. We would have a play area in back with things to climb on and enough room for picnics and summer parties. I'd make mom's famous chocolate cake. You would cook steaks and hot dogs. Our home would ring with laughter.*

And with thoughts of regret, Sally returned to the house to get ready for the movers, set to arrive in a couple of hours. When she closed the door for the last time her future would begin. One in which she directed her life, not followed someone else's plan.

The End

Author's Note

When I begin a book I write for myself. The characters and twists and turns in the plot are created to keep me turning the page. However, you the reader have spent time in the worlds I have created, so I welcome your thoughts. They provide guidance for those stories yet to be told.

For those of you who have enjoyed reading *What She Didn't Know*, I ask you to write a review and post it on Amazon for other readers to find.

Thank you in advance.

Patricia E. Gitt

Made in the USA
Middletown, DE
30 April 2021